PENGUIN BOOKS

LAW SCHOOL

A graduate of Wesleyan University and the University of Virginia School of Law, Arthur T. Vanderbilt, II, clerked for an appellate judge before serving as Deputy Attorney General of New Jersey and counsel to the New Jersey Board of Public Utilities and Department of Energy. He later served as Assistant Counsel to the Governor of New Jersey. Mr. Vanderbilt is now associated with the New Jersey and New York law firm Kraft & Hughes and specializes in municipal bond work. He is active in Republican politics in New Jersey. Mr. Vanderbilt is also the author of *Changing Law*, which was a selection of the Lawyers Literary Club and won the American Bar Association's award as the best book about the law published in 1976; *Jersey Justice: Three Hundred Years of the New Jersey Judiciary*; and articles and book reviews for legal periodicals.

LAW
SCHOOL

Briefing for a
Legal Education

by Arthur T. Vanderbilt, II

PENGUIN BOOKS

PENGUIN BOOKS
Published by the Penguin Group
Viking Penguin Inc., 40 West 23rd Street,
New York, New York, 10010, U.S.A.
Penguin Books Ltd, 27 Wrights Lane,
London W8 5TZ England
Penguin Books Australia Ltd, Ringwood,
Victoria, Australia
Penguin Books Canada Ltd, 2801 John Street,
Markham, Ontario, Canada L3R 1B4
Penguin Books (N.Z.) Ltd, 182–190 Wairau Road,
Auckland 10, New Zealand

Penguin Books Ltd, Registered Offices:
Harmondsworth, Middlesex, England

First published in the United States of America
under the title *An Introduction to the Study of Law*
by Gann Law Books 1979
Published in Penguin Books 1981

5 7 9 10 8 6 4

LIBRARY OF CONGRESS CATALOGING IN PUBLICATION DATA
Vanderbilt, Arthur T   1950–
Law school.
Reprint of the 1979 ed. published under title: An
introduction to the study of law.
Includes bibliographical references and index.
I.   Law—Study and teaching—United States.   2.   Law
students—United States—Handbooks, manuals, etc.
I.   Title.
KF283.V36   1981   349.73'07'11   81-655
ISBN 0 14 00.5916 4   AACR1

Printed in the United States of America by
George Banta Co., Inc., Harrisonburg, Virginia
Set in Caledonia

CONTENTS

Introduction

Lawyers have never been universally popular. In fact, they have often been held in rather low esteem. Plato spoke of the "small and unrighteous" souls of lawyers. Jeremy Bentham, himself a lawyer, remarked that "lawyers are harpies of the law who poison the language to fleece their clients." Keats was somewhat less generous: "I think," he wrote, "we may class the lawyers in the natural history of monsters." And Shakespeare, in his classic line from *Henry VI*, Part II, suggested a rather drastic solution to the world's legal problems: "The first thing we do, let's kill all the lawyers." Times never change. A recent Harris poll rating public confidence in sixteen institutions found law firms at the bottom.[1]

Yet, despite the fact that lawyers have never been subject to mass affection, despite the fact that, in the words of Chief Judge Irving R. Kaufman of the United States Court of Appeals for the Second Circuit, "no other profession is subject to the public contempt and derision that sometimes befalls lawyers,"[2] students have always been attracted to the study of law. When Oliver Wendell Holmes, Jr., announced his decision to enter law school, his distinguished father asked, "What is the use of that, Wendell? A lawyer can't be a great man."[3] The career of the great jurist, of course, answered his father's fears.

Today, college students seem to have little question about the desirability of practicing law. In the past fifteen years, law school enrollments have more than doubled, from 54,000 to 126,000. Each year approximately 40,000 college students enter law school and each year about 30,000 law school graduates are admitted to the bar as new attorneys. During the last decade, the number of lawyers in the United States has increased from 296,000 to 462,000.[4] Any reservations college students might harbor about the wisdom of pursuing a legal education would seem to be outweighed by their observation of the leading roles lawyers play in the community, the state, and the nation, or by their conception of the law as a gateway to politics, business, or other forms of power in an increasingly complex society of laws. Despite the bruised public image of lawyers, it cannot be doubted that the professional class described by de Tocqueville as "the American aristocracy" is still alive and well.

But, for all the eagerness with which each new class of college graduates begins the study of law, students remain, for the most part, ignorant of what a legal education entails, how best to study law, and what precisely the practice of law is all about. As a result, it would almost seem to be a truism that a student's introduction to the study of law will be a troubled time of confusion and uncertainty. The first year of law school, a time of disorientation if not mystification, has always been the legal profession's common experience, the first trial the law student must win in order to become a lawyer.

Many are the tales that are told by those who stumbled at the threshold of the study of law, or who initially felt the law to be a strange domain, quite apart from ordinary life. Patriot and president John Adams found the study of law in the eighteenth century "a dreary ramble,"[5] as did Supreme Court Justice William Paterson, who, on looking back at his student days, was convinced that the law, "especially at first, is a disagreeable study."[6] Justice Joseph Story as a student "cried over the gnarled prose of Lord Coke,"[7] whose treatises were basic texts of the day. In the next century, novelist Henry James reported that he "sat through the first year's lectures at Harvard Law School and quit in despair because he could not understand, he said, one word of what the lecturer said or what the books said."[8] Poet-author-physician Oliver Wendell Holmes was also repelled from the law, likening it to "sawdust without butter." "If you can eat sawdust without butter," he counseled his son, you will be a success in the law."[9] Oliver Wendell Holmes, Jr., reported after his first classes at law school that he "could not make sense of one word."[10] More recently, Felix Frankfurter revealed that he had been so frightened at law school that he could not recall speaking up "at all during the first year."[11] And famed criminal lawyer F. Lee Bailey, on thinking back to his law student days, remembered "the work . . . and the many nights without sleep, and the cramming to get through an exam. . . . And there was always the tension."[12]

Taught law may well be tough law, and law schools may make tough law, as F. W. Maitland remarked,[13] but the period of unrelieved confusion during the first year of law school seems an unnecessary and outmoded rite of passage. The first year at law school is the year with the greatest formative effect on the professional life of a young lawyer. It is then that he should acquire the lawyer's ability to absorb facts and rules accurately and quickly, to search for the controlling reasons for a rule of law, to employ these rules in hypothetical situations, to acquire the capacity for hard, prolonged intellectual labor, and to develop a genuine interest in the law as an important aspect of life. As it is, no law school can hope in the three years at its disposal to teach a student all that he will need to know for a life as an enlightened member of the legal profession. It is, therefore, unfortunate that all too often most of a student's first year in law school—one third of his formal legal education—is spent trying to discover the correct approach to the study of law. It was with these thoughts in mind that I prepared the Studying Law section of this book as a guide for the first-year student on the special requirements of a legal education, and so, as a manual on how to succeed in law school.

With this section I have included two essays written by my grandfather. From his varied perspectives as a trial and appellate lawyer, a law professor and Dean of the New York University School of Law, a President of the American Bar Association and of the American Judicature Society, and as Chief Justice of New Jersey,[14] he had a unique opportunity to observe the effectiveness of the training provided by law schools. The 1950 essays reprinted here concern Prelegal Education and the Art of Advocacy. Together, the three sections provide the student contemplating a legal career and the student about to begin law school with an introduction to the study of law.

The first section, on Prelegal Education, is concerned with the faculties that are involved in the study and practice of law and the course of study the prospective law student should undertake in preparation for law school and his work as a lawyer. As the law is but an aspect of life, any course a student takes or any extracurricular activity in which he engages may—as practicing lawyers know from experience—be unexpectedly useful someday. But some indication of what interests, training, and subjects are most likely to aid in law school and in the practice of law can help in planning the best possible education for those training toward the law.

All too often, students come from college to law school quite unprepared for the kind of work that is carried on there. The second section, Studying Law, is a practical guide for achieving a successful law school record. By knowing what to expect from law school and by understanding the basic mechanical aspects involved in the study of law, the student will be in a position immediately to apply his talents to the work at hand. And, it cannot but be helpful for the prospective law student to learn while still in secondary school or college that the work of law school will be quite different from his earlier educational experiences. The prospective law student may intelligently begin preparing for graduate studies by seeing hcw the law schools go about preparing their students for the practice of law and by knowing in advance what law school is like.

Although lawyers are engaged in a wide variety of professional activities, in the final analysis the development of the law and the professional work of every lawyer depends on the work of the advocate. It is the advocate representing his client in court, before an administrative agency or before a legislative body, who is at the frontier of where the law is made, or at least declared, and whose work determines the direction the law will take. Thus, the basic elements involved in the work of every lawyer who deals with clients stand out most clearly and to the highest degree in the work of the advocate. The final section, The Art of Advocacy, presents an analysis of the work of the lawyer as advocate so that the student may see what aptitudes, skills, and knowledge are required or are advantageous in the practice of law. With such an analysis as a blueprint, the student may decide how best to develop or acquire them, both as a prelaw and as a law student. And the student will begin to understand to some extent the relationship of law school studies to the attainment of particular professional goals.

Many, on their first approach to the study of law, have felt themselves repelled by what Edward Gibbon called "the thorns and thickets of that gloomy labyrinth." For those who are contemplating a future in the legal profession and for those who are about to commence the study of law, this book has been designed as a guide through what has seemed a veritable *terra incognita*. With such an Ariadne's thread to follow, the law will hopefully prove to be neither so labyrinthine nor so gloomy as it might otherwise, on first impression, have seemed. And with a more complete understanding of what the study of law is all about, the student's formal legal education may be not only more profitable, but also more enjoyable.

LAW
SCHOOL

Prelegal Education

The pilot of an airplane or of a ship has a much better chance of reaching his destination safely and with less mental strain if he has a chart of his course than if he has to cruise without any guide except his native ingenuity. In like fashion, the student, whether in high school or college, who contemplates the study of law will have a safer voyage if he has a chart of his educational course.

The very first question he has to ask himself is, "What is my destination? Is it to gain admittance to a recognized law school and to graduate from it? Or is it to be admitted to the bar and to practice law successfully? Or is it in addition to all of these things to become a well-rounded person and citizen, a leader in the affairs of his community, state, or country?" These ports are not located in opposite directions. They lie very much along the same route. But the length of the voyage to each port and the amount of preparation therefor differ—as do the rewards, tangible and intangible, to be obtained both en route and on arrival. Each student must select his own goal. For the ambitious and public-spirited student, the choice is clearly indicated.

Increasingly the courses in college and law school alike are being organized for the benefit of the student who aspires not merely to earn a living in his profession but to make a genuine contribution to it—who aims to use his talents not exclusively for himself but for society as well. And this is certainly as it should be, for there never was a time when leaderhip both in public and private affairs was at a higher premium.

There is unfortunately no place to which the student may resort to obtain an authoritative map to guide him to his port of destination. Life has never been completely charted and probably never will be, and law is but an aspect of life. But this does not mean that he need lack substantial guidance: (1) He may have spread out before him an outline of the work of the lawyer so that he may in a sense see for himself what aptitudes, skills, and knowledge are required or are advantageous in the practice of the profession. (2) In this connection it will be well for him to know, in a general way at least, how the law schools aim to prepare the student for the practice of law, for the law school will be his first port of call after college. It will be helpful for him to learn that the work in law school is quite different from the work in most colleges and that all too often students come from college to law school quite unprepared for the kind of instruction carried on there. (3) He may have exhibited to him what the leaders in the several branches of the profession think is the best route to his destination and what training and equipment he requires for his voyage. (4) And finally, we have available the advice of some of the great judges and statesmen of the latter part of the eighteenth century.

Why, it may be asked, should we go back over a century and a half for confirmation of what is needed for the education of a lawyer now? The answer is simple: It was the age of the American Revolution, the French Revolution, and the Industrial Revolution. The world was being made over economically, politically, socially, and to a degree intellectually. Can anyone who is familiar with world history of the past thirty years doubt that we are living in an age of revolution? "Permanent Revolution," one distinguished scholar has called it.[1] In such periods the law as well as society changes rapidly, and this calls for far greater ability in the legal profession than in ordinary times, when routine and precedent will suffice. It calls for men like Washington and Hamilton, Adams and Jefferson in statecraft, like Madison among Constitution makers and Marshall among Constitution interpreters, like Kent and Story among the men who adapted the common law to the needs of a young country. It calls for men like Lord Mansfield, who demonstrated the power of a judge to adopt the common law to the needs of a new age, for men like Bentham, the great law reformer, and Blackstone, whose *Commentaries*, Burke tells us, were as much read here as in England. The two ages have too much in common for us to neglect the advice of these great men.

THE WORK OF THE LAWYER

What then, is the nature of a lawyer's work? Lawyers carry on a wide variety of activities but in the final analysis the advocate representing his client in court typifies the profession, for it is in the courts and other tribunals that the rights which the law protects must be vindicated. Sir William Osler, the great physician, once said: "The worst thing about quacks is that they cure people." The advocate is in no such danger of unmerited success; there are always two lawyers in court ready, willing, and generally able to expose any weakness in his position—his adversary and the judge. The test of the advocate is very real and always immediate. He must be prepared to bring all of his forces into action at a moment's notice. It will not avail him to know the facts of his case or the rules of law applicable thereto tomorrow.

The efforts of a lawyer in court, whether trying a case before

a judge and a jury, or a judge alone, or arguing an appeal
before a group of judges, are but a small part of his work on his
case or his appeal. Like an iceberg, only one ninth shows.
Before a lawyer goes to court he must have heard his client's
story, read the documents in the case, interviewed the witnesses, looked up the law, drafted his pleadings, studied his
adversary's pleadings, conducted examinations before trial,
perhaps have answered interrogatories, prepared a trial brief,
and attended a pretrial conference before the judge with opposing counsel. On an appeal he has a record of the trial below
to study, the law to look up, a brief to prepare, an answering
brief of his adversary to reply to, an oral argument to outline,
all before he makes his brief argument in court—and the
briefer it is, the more difficult his task. When Woodrow Wilson was asked how long it took him to prepare a speech, he
replied that he required two months to work up a twenty-
minute speech, a month for a half-hour speech, but an hour
speech he was prepared to make on call.

It is important that the prospective law student see that at
every step the lawyer is dealing with three very different
things—rules of law, which are abstract; facts, which are specific; and persons, each of whom is, whatever else may be said
of him, a very complex individual. This diversity of subject
matter is typical not only of the court work of the lawyer, but
of his office work as well. As the counsellor of his clients he is
always dealing with abstract rules, concrete facts, complex personalities. Moreover, he does not deal with these abstract
rules, these concrete facts, these complex personalities in a
vacuum. He deals with them in their physical, social, and
intellectual environment. Advice, for example, that would be
sound in ordinary circumstances would be quite inadequate in
the presence of an army, be it friendly or hostile. The significance of environment is heightened when the lawyer under-
takes to act for more than individual clients, for groups, incor-
porated or not, public or private. It reaches its highest point

when he is chosen to act as a legislator or chief magistrate, whether of his town, county, state, or country. But his environment in the broad sense of the term, whether he is acting for a private client or the nation, is always in his mind as a factor.

These four factors in a lawyer's work—abstract rules, specific facts, complex personalities, and environment, which he is likely to refer to as the "social order"—suggest the training and the subjects that may well engage the attention of the future law student. In this connection it should be observed that almost every action of a lawyer involves all four of these factors. It will avail the law student little to master any three of these factors if he ignores the fourth. It is of little value to know how to start an automobile if one does not also understand how to steer it and stop it—and know the rules of the road. It should be noted, too, what diverse qualities of mind are called for by these four elements of a lawyer's work. Abstractions call for the faculties of the thinker, but the thinking relates to the practical affairs of men, the avoidance of strife, the promotion of order, the doing of justice. Facts, on the other hand, are the common property of all, ranging from the simple facts of everyday life to the precise facts of science. There is almost no limit to the range of facts—material, intellectual, spiritual—that may engage the attention of the lawyer. The art, natural or acquired, of knowing and dealing with people is a third sphere that seems remote from logic and philosophy, from mathematics and science. It brings to mind rather the boys' club, the athletic field, the discussions around the dining room table at home, the "bull sessions" in the college fraternity house, the varied activities of the campus, the daily newspaper, the people one has met at school or on vacation—yes, and the books one has read and the plays one has seen. Psychology has its uses, but psychology never taught a man how to pick a jury.

The fourth factor, environment, covers more than politics,

economics, and sociology, though it includes all of them. It deals as well with the ideas and the ideals that move men. Ideas and ideals are born, grow, bear fruit—and sometimes die. To understand them, as well as to understand politics, economics, and sociology, we must know history. Most of all the lawyer must know the age-old struggle between the power of government and the freedom of the individual—a conflict fought now on one ground, now on another, but always being fought, if people are to preserve their liberty. The larger the interests a lawyer represents, private or public, the more important it is that he have a broad knowledge of his environment.

The lawyer must be able to think in terms of facts, of persons, of the abstractions we call law, and of environment. It is the variety of the factors with which he works daily that adds so much to the zest of his life. But he must also be able to express his thoughts in words. The abstractions we call law and the lawyer's notions of facts are unintelligible to us except in words. These words he must adapt to the capacity of the people with whom he is dealing. In short, the lawyer must know how to speak and write clearly and interestingly. Much of a lawyer's life is spent in handling words. They are a large part of his environment. He must master them or they will master him. He must know their full meaning—their definition, connotation, and associations. Otherwise he is indeed a "mute inglorious Milton." This factor of spoken and written expression, then, is a fifth aspect of a lawyer's work. Many unthinking people would put it first: they are impressed by a person's presence, the flash of his eye, his silver tongue, the honeyed words that soothe and charm. All this is splendid and in some places it may carry all before it, but regardless of his eloquence, if a lawyer does not know his law, the judge will rule against him, and if he does not know his facts his adversary will expose his ignorance. The cultivation of the power of expression is worth much time, thought, and effort. This effort to phrase his law and to explain his facts takes up a considerable part of his thought, but with a real lawyer language is always a means, never the end.

The work of the advocate, it will be seen, consists essentially in aiding in the solving of problems—the problems of human beings, singly or collectively, with reference to their rights and responsibilities in a very real world. Problem-solving also is the function of the other branches of the profession. They, too, must face reality in a very practical way. The counsellor advising his client, whether a poor widow or a rich corporation, whether some public body or an unincorporated association like a labor union, must apply the abstractions he calls law to specific facts, must deal with people and their rights in the light of the social order, must give his advice in understandable English—and must be prepared to see it tested out in court.

The judge is likewise concerned with all five factors. If he is a good judge, he will be concerned in particular with the conflict that so often appears between what actually is, what ideally ought to be, and what the law says officially must be if penalties are not to follow. The "is," the "ought to be," and the "must, or else," it should be added, are likewise in the advocate's mind, for law from one standpoint, as Mr. Justice Holmes has pointed out, is "the prophecies of what the courts will do in fact."[2] Like the advocate's pleadings and motions, like the counsellor's opinions, the trial judge's rulings are subject to scrutiny, in his case by an appellate court. And even the work of the highest courts in the land is subject to the criticism of both popular and professional opinion, forces far more potent than many students at first realize. It follows then that the power of self-criticism is of great importance to the lawyer, if he would avoid criticism elsewhere—and defeat.

This applies not only to the advocate, the counsellor, and the judge, but also to the legislator, the chief executive, and the administrator. If the legislator falls down in incorporating sound rules of law in his statute or bases it on insufficient facts, if one or the other of these elements collides too violently with its environment or runs counter to human nature or is expressed in inept language, he may expect both popular and professional criticism and possible defeat. So, too, with the executive and the administrator. All must measure up or expect deserved criticism.

HOW LAW IS STUDIED

From this discussion of the chief elements that enter into the work of the lawyer, in whatever branch of the profession he may be employed, the prospective law student may infer in a general way what college studies and training will be of most value in preparation for the practice of law. A brief description of the work of the modern law student will throw additional light on the matter and perhaps modify his first impressions.

In the law schools textbooks, if not entirely taboo, are at least of very subordinate importance. From his very first day the law student works with the very same material that he will use all his life as a lawyer—the reported decisions of the courts and other tribunals, and constitutions, legislation, regulations, and ordinances. From his first day on he will use source material rather than somebody's statements about those sources.

Each reported case he studies will give him the facts of the case, the contentions of the rival parties, the issue between the parties as developed in their contending statements or pleadings, the decision of the court on the issue, and the reasons assigned by the court for the decision. Involuntarily his reasoning powers are called into play: Is the decision right? Is the reason for the decision sound? He compares it with another case which seems to enunciate an opposite ruling. Are the two decisions really contradictory? Or can they be reconciled? Similar queries suggest themselves as to the reasons assigned by the courts for the decisions. The instructor's first question is likely to be, "Do you agree with the case? Is the decision right?" The student is then face to face with the very same question which confronts a judge in every case that comes before him with all of its practical, legal and ethical implications. The instructor in due time may put to the class a hypothetical case and ask for a student's opinion on it. Or he may change a single fact in a case, and then ask if the change alters the decision, in the student's opinion. Judges have a way of bringing into a case statements of law that have no application to the issue in hand. Such a statement is *obiter dictum*, something said by the way, or dictum, as lawyers call it more briefly. The instructor will soon inquire whether a particular statement of law in an opinion is the ground of the decision, the *ratio decidendi*, and so controlling, or is it mere dictum?

In this process of reading a case and discussing the opinion of the court, the law student is dealing with the specific facts of the case, with the people therein, with the rule of law applicable thereto, with the environment of the case, and throughout with language—the five factors in a lawyer's work. It is all as real as life itself. It is contentious. The attitude is one of "show me." No authority is too high to be questioned. As Mr. Justice Story, one of the greatest justices of the United States Supreme Court, put it to his law school students:

> Gentlemen, this is the High Court of Errors and Appeals from all other courts in the world. Tell me not of the last cited case having overruled any great principle—not at all. Give me the *principle*, even if you find it laid down in the Institutes of Hindu Law.[3]

Out of all this study and discussion the student writes his notebooks, which in a very real sense are his own textbooks on the law of the different subjects he is studying. They are his own because they arise out of his experience. In all of his study and discussion, in class and out, one element predominates: Like the practicing lawyer or judge in actual controversies, he is using—and developing—his powers of reasoning.

Reasoning is the faculty that gives cohesion to his work as it does to the labors of the advocate and the judge. As his reasoning moves from facts or personalities or environment to or from law (using language, of course), he is weaving several very real worlds of experience together. It is the use of this faculty of reasoning that makes for much of the stimulation and enjoyment of his work both as a student and as a practitioner. The reasoning of the lawyer, it will be seen from the elements with which he deals, is not the reasoning of the logician, the mathematician, the scientist, or the philosopher, though there is much he may learn from them. His reasoning differs from each of theirs, as theirs, in turn, differs from that of the historian, the biographer, the economist, the sociologist, the accountant, and the statistician, from each of whom the law student may also gain much. As he studies his cases and reasons about them he comes to see what one of our greatest judges meant when he said:

The life of the law has not been logic; it has been experience. The felt necessities of the time, the prevalent moral and political theories, intentions of public policy, avowed or unconscious, even the prejudices which judges share with their fellowmen, have had a great deal more to do than the syllogism in determining the rules by which men should be governed. The law embodies the story of a nation's development through many centuries, and it cannot be dealt with as if it contained only the axioms and corollaries of a book of mathematics. In order to know what it is, we must know what it has been and what it tends to be. We must assuredly consult history and existing theories of legislation.[4]

So, highest among the factors with which the lawyer constantly works, we must place reasoning—not mere logic, but reasoning based on experience, what the great Lord Coke termed "the artificial reason and judgment of the law."

Education in which reasoning predominates is nothing new. It is as old as Socrates and it is described by Plato in the *Republic:*

> Education is not at all what certain of its professors declare it to be. They tell us they put Knowledge into an empty soul, as though one should put sight into blind eyes. Our theory is quite another kind. [There is] this faculty of Reason present in every human soul, this organ wherewith each man learns. . . . Education is therefore the art of converting the Reason.

The reason is "converted" not by lectures or books but by informal discussion provoked by the instructor's questions. This way of teaching in which thinking is emphasized over mere learning owes its renaissance in American legal education to the wisdom of a great educational innovator, President Charles W. Eliot of Harvard, in sensing the weakness of lectures and textbooks in training real lawyers and in seeking out Christopher Columbus Langdell as Dean of the Law School. To Langdell we owe the case system of studying law. He combined the study of original sources (the method of modern science) with the Socratic tradition of question and answer. The combination is an ideal one from the standpoint of developing the legal ability of the student. Each case involves at least one question which has to be answered, and the student is obliged to compare his answer with the court's or his fellow student's, or the instructor's solution of the problem.

The student's approach to the study of his cases is that of the judge rather than that of the attorney. The judge strives for impartiality and the truth as between the contending parties. First he has to decide, in many cases where there is no jury, as between the rival contentions of the parties, what the facts of the case actually are. This is by no means an easy task in the face of conflicting testimony from witnesses of varying degrees of credibility. In dealing with facts, the more he knows of life and human nature, of the arts and sciences, the better; and the greater his skill in acquiring knowledge and marshalling facts, as a general assembles and arranges his army, the better his legal work. This ability to grasp and master facts is a prime requisite of the law student, the lawyer, and the judge.

Next the judge has to weigh the conflicting views of the parties as to the law. Here he is frequently referred by counsel to what appear to be divergent decisions. Often they are not so in fact. If they are not, he must carefully distinguish them. When the decisions actually are in conflict, he must decide which ones are sound in principle and wise in practice. To do this he must know not only the single pertinent rule of law, but its correlated rules and their controlling principles. The law student must follow the same process. By patient research and much discussion he extracts from the cases the rules and principles of law and welds them into a harmonious whole in his own notebook In this, too, as Mr. Justice Holmes so clearly demonstrated, the more the student knows of history and of his political economic, social, and moral environment, the more likely is his decision to be correct. In short, the more comprehensive the student's grasp of life and of human nature, as well as of the arts and sciences, the more effective will be his work in the law. This statement, we must hasten to add, is subject to two important provisos: First, he must be able to put his knowledge to use practically in his reasoning; and secondly, he must be able to express himself. Without these faculties it would be useless for him to have available encyclopedic information, for the practice of law is nothing if not a practical art.

Enough has been said, however, to emphasize, if emphasis is still necessary, the need of the law school student's having a very wide background of knowledge of life and its arts and sciences; of his being able to use his knowledge, *i.e.*, reason about it; of his being able to express himself adequately; and of his being able to acquire information and marshal it skillfully

and speedily. With such a wide background of educati[
reading of every case will add to his knowledge of life as well
as of law, *i.e.*, will augment his liberal education; without it,
his reading of the cases will lose much of its significance. The
truth of this statement may readily be tested by any prospective law student. Read carefully any one of Chief Justice Marshall's great opinions. Next read the story of that particular
decision in Beveridge's *Life of John Marshall*. Then reread the
case and ask yourself if you really understood the Chief Justice
on the first reading.

It is worth repeating that law is an aspect of life and accordingly as broad as life itself. The pace in law school is so fast and
the amount of ground to be covered so extensive that it is
inescapable that the student who knows how to reason and
how to express himself, who knows something of human nature, who understands at least in broad outline his environment—physical, social, and moral—and who knows how to
assemble information rapidly and accurately has a great advantage over the student who is deficient in one or another of
these particulars. For the well-prepared student, each case he
reads is a continuation of his liberal education, for law properly
studied by a properly prepared student is just as much liberal
education as any subject in the college curriculum. Thus
studied and taught, law is worthy of a place in a university, but
not otherwise.

RECOMMENDATIONS OF THE LEADERS
OF THE PROFESSION

Our analysis of the work of the lawyer into its component
factors and our résumé of how law is studied, with training in
reasoning emphasized as the fundamental element, will, it is
hoped, give added significance to the recommendations of
leaders of the profession to the prospective law student.

It is clear that prelegal education is more than a matter of certain courses or of particular extracurricular activities or even of a certain number of years of study. This point of view is forcibly expressed by Chief Justice Harlan F. Stone, whose words have especial force not merely by reason of his judicial and legal experience but also because of his many years of outstanding service as dean of one of the leading law schools of the country:

I have no doubt that in general members of the Bar should have much more prelegal education than is usually the case at the present time. But this does not necessarily mean that they should have more years of training or take more or different courses.

I think the usual college course is little enough prelegal training for the man who aspires to become a competent member of the Bar. But even that period of study does not necessarily mean that it will make him an educated man or properly qualify him to take up law study. Men who come to the Bar should be equipped to stand on their own feet intellectually, to do their own thinking, with developed capacity to exercise an independent and critical judgment, such as can come only from a considerable period of intensive study and intellectual self-discipline. This is not wholly a matter of years, of hours, or courses. It depends much more on the predilections of the student himself and the kind of training he has had, including his self-directed reading and thinking, quite as much as the courses he has taken and the number of hours or years he has spent in taking them. If his reading and study have been carried on under a guidance and with methods which incite his intellectual curiosity and develop his intellectual self-reliance, the result ought to be, in the case of those of fair mental equipment, that they leave college with the marks of an educated man, the inclination and trained capacity to form considered and enlightened judgments upon most of the problems involved in the art of living in civilized society. Whether he will get this kind of intellectual experience in his classes in Hebrew, or in mathematics, or history, or economics, or a judicious selection from all, depends upon the man himself and the kind of guidance he gets in the courses he selects rather than his particular selection of subjects without reference to the manner in which they are given. Therefore it seems to me that . . . the emphasis should be put on the intellectual discipline which the student derives from courses and by particular teachers, rather than to the selection of particular subjects without reference to the way in which they are taught. If the student is so advised and has the intelligence needful to a good lawyer he may be depended upon to make the best use of the facilities which his college affords.

Of course the student should get a certain amount of information which is the subject matter of the thinking of his time. But it is a mistake to suppose that he will be an educated man or a good lawyer merely because he has gained a certain accumulation of information, however it may be distributed over the college curriculum.

Nor do I think it is greatly important whether he takes all the selected college courses before he begins law study, or some of them concurrently with it. The notion that it is *necessary* to take economics, sociology and the like at the same time as taking law in order to get a proper approach to legal problems, seems to me utterly fallacious. If the law student has had satisfactory prelegal training, that will be best accomplished by placing in the professors' chairs in law schools men who see the relationship of those subjects to law and value it at its true worth.

Next to be observed is an *opposition to required courses* in prelegal training. Students do their best work in subjects in which they are vitally interested:

> No profit grows where is no pleasure ta'en,
> In brief, Sir, study which you most affect.

An inspired teacher, moreover, in a subject relatively remote from the law can do more to help a student by awakening his intellectual processes than a poor instructor in a subject that touches the law more closely. Many lawyers, too, came forward with concrete instances of the utility in the trials of their cases of subjects that seem far removed from actual practice—chemistry, art, biology—nor is this strange, for the practice of law may be as broad as life. Many of our best students, furthermore, do not make up their minds to study law until late in college—they may be juniors or seniors before their interest is kindled—and it would be a great loss to society to bar these students from the law by a required prelegal curriculum. On the other hand, the prospective lawyer should not concentrate unduly on one subject or in one field, nor diffuse his efforts in too many directions. A wide range of interests must be reconciled with deep experience. The law schools have learned that only by putting training in thinking first can they harmonize these seemingly conflicting aims.

Of paramount importance is a genuine, vital interest in the intellectual world and training in thinking and expression above the acquisition of mere knowledge. In this process the significance of *the great teacher* and ultimately of *self-education* as being the soundest kind of education is repeatedly stressed. Lawyers are not likely to lose sight of the fact that in the last analysis everything depends on the individual and that it is the individual who must train and discipline himself. Intelligence cannot be taught, but it can be acquired. Interest, capacity to work, and health are all indispensable aids in the process, but sound habits and a wise use of time are no less necessary to that end.

Important also are such extracurricular activities as develop capacity for independent thought and action, especially when they involve training in expression. As Judge Charles E. Clark of the United States Circuit Court of Appeals for the Second Circuit, formerly Dean of Yale Law School, aptly put it:

These extracurricular activities may often have more vitality than the college work itself, especially if the latter is soft and limited to lectures. Those positions requiring responsibility, executive ability and leadership are of course the most important.

Professor Karl N. Llewellyn of Columbia Law School set forth a list of skills and interests a student should bring to law school and the subjects that may help him, both of which are well worth quoting:

What I want a student to bring to law school from college has more to do with results than with subject matter: ability to (1) read; (2) write; (3) use a library; (4) evaluate opinion and evidence; (5) evaluate opinion and evidence quantitatively as well as qualitatively; (6) size up people. And interest in doing all of these.

There is little use trying to prescribe subject-matter for acquisition of such skills and interests. It is a matter of temperament and teaching. And the skills and interests are more important than any subject-matter. But I should prefer somewhat to have the stuff on which a student exercised himself while acquiring the skills, include:

(a) Descriptive (not theoretical) economics, and economic history;

(b) Political, social, and constitutional history, first, of the United States; second, of some other people or culture. And practice in the interpretation of documentary evidence seems to me particularly desirable;

(c) Some sociological study of modern America. Or some technological study of it. Or both;

(d) Some quantitative science or art; physics, or quantitative chemistry, statistical operations in economic or sociological data, or (as in accounting) in dollars.

(e) Art, or literature;

(f) Psychology, or heredity, or anthropo-geography; *i.e.*, at least one of the disciplines which indicate the limits of what manipulation of, or by the environment, can accomplish;

(g) Descriptive politics. Not "political science."

He concluded to the same effect as Judge Clark:

> It is to be noted that the extracurricular game of jockey-
> ing for office and the like will often bring a man farther
> than study of this list of subject-matter, when it comes to
> seeing how and why courts do what they do, and what to
> do about it.[5]

In short, a lawyer must know people and his environment and
how to cope with both. Books and thinking are fine—but they
are not enough.

Some of the subjects in a curriculum may sound distasteful
to some students. They may even bring to mind Mr. Dooley's
dictum, "It doesn't make much difference what you study, so
long as you don't like it." It should be borne in mind that
while the leaders of the profession, and lawyers generally, are
opposed to prescribing required subjects for the prospective
law student, they nevertheless realize the necessity for discipline in accurate thinking, in clear expression and in a sound
understanding of our physical, social, intellectual, and moral
environment as well as a deep knowledge of human nature. It
is for the student himself to decide in the light of all this
advice whether he is willing to pay the price in time and effort
that these studies demand in order to become a lawyer. An
even more difficult decision to make is whether the instructors
in his college in each recommended subject are capable of
arousing his enthusiasm. And most difficult of all is the problem of whether or not to pursue a recommended subject even
with an uninspiring instructor.

If the student, having been fully advised to take a particular
course, fails to do so, the burden is then on him to use his own
ingenuity to make up his lack. "It is superstition that is all too
persistent," to quote Professor Zechariah Chafee, Jr., "to suppose that it is necessary to take a course in a subject to know
something about it. A chief count in the indictment against
college education is that it fails to develop a desire for reading

books in fields outside the courses."[6] Intellectual fire is more likely to be kindled in a subject freely chosen, under proper advice, than in a compulsory course.

In all of his work the prospective law student will do well to keep in mind the wisdom of rare old Ben Jonson:

> It is not growing like a tree
> In bulk, doth make man better be.

Knowledge is only worthwhile when it has been assimilated and thus made usable. The capacity to work hard, the ability to think straight, training in expressing oneself well both orally and in writing, the understanding of and sympathy with people one meets, a social consciousness, a keen interest in life, all are more important than any amount of knowledge. The student will do well to seek out instructors who promise him training and inspiration along with knowledge rather than knowledge for its own sake.

CONFIRMATION FROM THE ELDER STATESMEN

We are living in a revolutionary age. The velocity of social change is greater than in any earlier era of English or American history and this has inevitably put a great strain on the law. The relation of the individual and the state, especially, is in a condition of flux. The period in our history that most nearly compares with present times is the era of the American Revolution, the French Revolution, and the English Industrial Revolution of a century and three quarters ago. The lawyers of this earlier revolutionary period, whether as judges or as statesmen, showed remarkable wisdom and skill in adapting the law of their day to a rapidly changing economic, political, social, and intellectual environment. Their success has been unrivaled in any other period of the long history of the common law, largely by reason of their boundless confidence in facing their problems and coping with them by their powers of reasoning. In their reasoning they did not neglect the wisdom of the past; they were great believers in a liberal education. It is therefore not without significance to note that the advice given to law students by the great judges and statesmen of what is often referred to as the Golden Age of the Law parallels that given by the leaders of the profession today.

To a young lawyer who wrote him for advice, Chancellor Kent, the author of the *Commentaries on American Law,* who has been called the father of American equity, wrote:

> At the June Circuit in 1786, I saw Ed. Livingstone (now the codifier for Louisiana) & he had a pocket Horace & read some passages to me at some office & pointed out their beauties, assuming that I well understood Horace. I said nothing, but was stung with shame & mortification, for I had forgotten even my Greek letters. I purchased immediately Horace and Virgil, a dictionary & grammar, and a Greek Lexicon & grammar and the testament, & formed my resolution promptly and decidedly to recover the lost languages. . . .
>
> From 1788 to 1798 I steadily divided the day into five portions, & alloted them to Greek, Latin, law and business, French & English. I mastered the best of the Greek, Latin and French classics, & as well as the best English & law books at hand & read Machivael & all collateral branches of English history.[7]

No American lawyer today could give merely a fifth of his time to law and business and the other four fifths to literature. Indeed he would be fortunate if he could reverse the figures and give one fifth of his time to literature. So it behooves him, if he would have the equipment of a Kent, to make at least a start during his college years.

Thomas Jefferson was profoundly interested in legal education. Under his auspices the first professorship of law in America was set up at the College of William and Mary two years before the fall of Yorktown, with the learned Chancellor George Wythe as Professor of Law and Police. Writing to a young friend from Paris in 1787 Jefferson said:

Mathematics, Natural philosophy, Natural history, Anatomy, Chemistry, Botany, will become amusements for your hours of relaxation, and auxiliaries to your principal studies. Precious and delightful ones they will be. As soon as such a foundation is laid in them as you may build on as you please hereafter, I suppose you will proceed to your main objects, Politics, Law, Rhetoric & History. . . . I have proposed to you to carry on the study of the law with that of Politics & History. Every political measure will forever have an intimate connection with the laws of the land; and he who knows nothing of these will always be perplexed & often foiled by adversaries having the advantage of that knowledge over him. . . . With respect to modern languages, French, as I have before observed, is indispensable. Next to this the Spanish is most important to an American. Our connection with Spain is already important & will become daily more so. Besides this the ancient part of American history is written chiefly in Spanish. To a person who would make a point of reading & speaking French & Spanish, I should doubt the utility of learning Italian. These three languages, being all degeneracies from the Latin, resemble one another so much that I doubt the possibility of keeping in the head a distinct knowledge of them all. . . . With your talents & industry, with science, and that steadfast honesty which eternally pursues right, regardless of consequences, you may promise yourself everything—but health, without which there is no happiness. An attention to health then should take place of every other object. The time necessary to secure this by active exercises, should be devoted to it in preference to every other pursuit.[8]

To another young friend, three years later, he wrote:

All that is necessary for a student is access to a library, and directions in what order the books are to be read. This I will take the liberty of suggesting to you, observing previously that as other branches of science, and especially history, are necessary to form a lawyer, these must be carried on together. I will arrange the books to be read in three columns, and propose that you should read those in the first column till 12. o'clock every day: those in the 2d. from 12. to 2. those in the 3d. after candlelight, leaving all the afternoon for exercise and recreation, which are as necessary as reading: I will rather say more necessary, because health is worth more than learning.[9]

Then come the three lists of books, in which there were as many historical works as law books, followed by some further advice:

Should there be any little intervals in the day not otherwise occupied fill them up by reading Lowthe's grammar, Blair's lectures on rhetoric, Mason on poetic & prosaic numbers, Bolingbroke's works for the sake of the style, which is declamatory & elegant, the English poets for the sake of style also.[10]

Some idea of the breadth of knowledge that John Adams thought appropriate for an educated man may be gleaned from a letter to Thomas Jefferson in 1814:

If I venture to give you my thoughts at all, they must be very crude. I have turned over Locke, Milton, Condillac, Rousseau, & even Miss Edgeworth, as a bird flies through the air. The "Preceptor" I have thought a good book. Grammar, rhetoric, logic, ethics, mathematics, cannot be neglected. Classics, in spite of our friend Rush, I must think indispensable. Natural history, mechanics, & experimental philosophy, chemistry, etc. at least their rudiments, cannot be forgotten. Geography, astronomy, & even history & chronology, though I am myself afflicted with a kind of pyrrhonism in the two latter, I presume cannot be omitted. Theology I would leave to Ray, Durham, Nieuwentyt, & Paley, rather than to Luther, Unzendorf, Swedenborg, Wesley, or Whitefield, or Thomas Aquinas, or Wollebius. Metaphysics I would leave in the clouds with the materialists and spiritualists, with Leibnitz, Berkeley, Prestley, & Edwards, &, I might add Hume & Reed. Or, if permitted to be read, it should be with romances & novels. What shall I say of music, drawing, fencing, dancing, & gymnastic exercises? What of languages, oriental or occidental? Of French, Italian, German, or Russian, of Sanscrit or of Chinese? The task you have prescribed to me of grouping these sciences or arts, under professors, within the view of an enlightened economy, is far beyond my forces. Loose, indeed, & undigested must be all the hints I can note.

Might grammar, logic & rhetoric be under one professor; Might mathematics, mechanics, & natural philosophy be under another? Geography & astronomy under a third? Laws & government, history & chronology, under a fourth? Classics might require a fifth.[11]

Mr. Justice Joseph Story, whose name, along with Kent's, would be included in a list of great American judges, devoted a considerable part of his inaugural address as Professor of Law at Harvard University to discussing the cultural requirements of the lawyer:

Many of our most illustrious statesmen have been lawyers, but they have been lawyers liberalized by philosophy, and a large intercourse with the wisdom of ancient and modern times. The perfect lawyer, like the perfect orator, must accomplish himself for his duties by familiarity with every study. It may be truly said, that to him nothing, that concerns human nature or human art, is indifferent or useless. He should search the human heart, and explore to their sources the passions, and appetites, and feelings of mankind. He should watch the motions of the dark and malignant passions, as they silently approach the chambers of the soul in its first slumbers. He should catch the first warm rays of sympathy and benevolence, as they play around the character, and are reflected back from its varying lines. He should learn to detect the cunning arts of the hypocrite, who pours into the credulous unwary ear his leperous distilment. He should for this purpose make the master-spirits of all ages pay contribution to his labors. He should walk abroad through nature, and elevate his thoughts, and warm his virtues, by a contemplation of her beauty, and magnificence, and harmony. He should examine well the precepts of religion, as the only solid basis of civil society; and gather from them, not only his duty, but his hopes; not merely his consolations, but his discipline and his glory. He should unlock all the treasures of history for illustration, and instruction, and admonition. He will thus see man, as he has been, and thereby best know what he is. He will thus be taught to distrust theory, and cling to practical good; to rely more upon experience than reasoning; more upon institutions than laws; more upon checks to vice than upon motives to virtue. He will become more indulgent to human errors; more scrupulous in means, as well as in ends; more wise, more candid, more forgiving, more disinterested. If the melancholy infirmities of his race shall make him trust men less, he may yet learn to love man more.[12]

Nor does he stop here. The student "must drink in the lessons and the spirit of philosophy . . . What has been already said rather presupposes than insists upon the importance of a full possession of the general literature of ancient and modern times."[13] Judge Story quotes with approval the advice given by Lord Chancellor Eldon, "I know of no rule to give them but that they must make up their mind to live like hermits and work like horses."[14] Most certainly may it be said that the American leaders of the profession in the post-Revolutionary period had standards of prelegal education that were fully as high as those recommended today.

Similar views were entertained by the great English judges.

Lord Mansfield, the great Chief Justice, whose name would be placed at the head of any list of English judges, in four letters published in the *European Magazine* for March 1791, and February, March and April 1792, gave "Directions for the Study of Ancient and Modern History Preparatory to the Study of the Law." While we shall not quote his advice at length, it should be noted that the student to whom his words were addressed was directed in considerable measure to original sources. He was referred to the History of Thucydides and advised to transcribe the speeches, such as the Funeral Oration made by Pericles, into his book. He was to "read over and over" the speeches of Demosthenes; "write observations into your book; get places that strike your imagination by heart. Reflect upon the nature of the Greek states; something like those of the Netherlands, Swiss, etc." Thus we have Lord Mansfield anticipating Maitland's "History involves comparison." Again, in dealing with Rome, the student was to read Sallust's History and Cicero's Orations. The student is referred to the *Lives of the Caesars* by Suetonius and to Tacitus.

Next, the student has his attention called to modern history. Here again the subject is viewed in a broad way, attention being directed particularly to the arts and literature. In dealing with English history Lord Mansfield starts with Caesar, Tacitus and Suetonius in the Roman period. Then come Jeffrey of Monmouth, William Malmesbury and Matthew Paris. And so on through every period of English history we have cited at every turn both contemporary sources and great literature:

> Collections of letters and state papers are of the utmost importance, if we pretend to exactness. . . . Sometimes a single pamphlet will give us better the clue of a transaction than a volume in folio. Thus we learn from the Duchess of Marlboro's apology that the peace of Utrecht was made by a quarrel between the women of the bedchamber: hence, memoirs, secret histories, political papers, etc., are not to be despised; always allowing sufficiently

for the prejudice of party, and believing them no farther than they are supported by collateral evidence.

His letter, dealing with a course of law studies, starts with general ethics and the law of nations:

For general ethics, which are the foundation of all law; read Xenophon's *memorabilia*, Tully's offices, and Woolaston's religion of nature. You may likewise look into Aristotle's ethics, which you will not like, but it is one of those books, *qui a limine salutandi sunt ne verba nobis dentur*.

For the law of nations, which is partly founded on the law of nature, and partly positive, read Grotius, and Pufendorf in Barbeyrac's translation, and Burlamaqui's *droit naturel;* as these authors treat the same subject in the heads, they may be read together and compared.

Then follow Roman law and Feudal law, the author concluding:

These writers are not sufficient to give you a thorough knowledge of the subjects they treat of; but they will give you general notions, general leading principles, and lay the best foundation that can be laid for the study of any municipal law; such as the law of England, Scotland, France, &c. &c.

Lord Chancellor Thurlow's advice to a young friend is no less thoroughgoing:

A good scholastic education founded upon grammar; and so much versification, as will give a taste for the best Greek and Latin poets, and Direct the Pronunciation of those languages, especially of the latter, which will frequently be wanted.

A residence at the University of Cambridge or Oxford for four years. In the first and second years, so much of

Euclid, Rutherford, and Locke, must be attended to, may be necessary for a general sketch of the mathematics, natural philosophy, and the rules of thinking; and with the less laborious and most agreeable improvements in the best classical authors, not forgetting the English writers.

In the third year, a close attention to chronology, geography, and history, both ancient and modern, with Campbell's state of Europe; the trade, interest, and policy, of neighboring nations.

In the fourth year, to learn French; to have a cursory view of Justinian's code and digest, and civil law; to take up the Roman history from time of Julius Caesar: get a general idea and knowledge of his expeditions into Gaul and Germany, and both invasions of Britain; collecting his anecdotes and customs of the people.

Then Tacitus de Moribus Germanorum, and De Vita Agricolai, then Selden's Janus Anglorum; then Wotton's Leges Walliae; then Wilkin's Leges Saxonicai; then Norman statutes in Russhead, with Magna Charta to the first of Richard I, when our Leges Non Scriptae are said to end, and statute law, pleadable as such, begins.

When the student is thus arrived at the beginning of our statute law, it will be soon enough for him to take up Blackstone.[15]

Lord Ashburton stresses classical attainments, the utility of Grammar, Rhetoric and Logic:

Geometry will afford the most apposite examples of close and pointed reasoning, and geography is so very necessary in common life, that there is less credit in knowing than dishonour in being unacquainted with it. But it is history, and more particularly that of his own country, which will occupy the attention, and attract the regard, of the great lawyer.[16]

The same volume from which these quotations are taken contains the "Reflections on the Natural and Acquired Endowments Requisite for the Study of Law" by Joseph Simpson, Esq. This work went through four editions in 1764, the year in which it was published. A mere listing of the subject headings will serve to demonstrate that the qualities required at the bar now have not changed in a century and a quarter: Perception, Memory, Judgment, Elocution, Learning, University Education, Study, Choice of Books, Taking Notes. Without qualification it may be stated that the advice of the American and English leaders of the profession of 175 years ago definitely conforms with the recommendations made by their successors of the present day as to the course of training the prospective law student should pursue.

CONCLUSIONS

Our analysis of the work of the lawyer and our description of the method of studying law will suggest to the alert student the subjects that should be studied in college, the faculties that should be trained, and the interest that should be aroused in preparation for the life of a lawyer. The task is one that demands the best efforts of the prospective lawyer. It calls for much more than mere book knowledge, although the lawyer, more than most other professions, relies on books. It requires genuine capacity for thinking, ability to master facts, deep knowledge of human nature, familiarity with his environment in the broadest sense of the term, ability to express his thoughts and feelings, and knowledge of himself acquired from the practice of self-criticism.

If the future lawyer finds, as he doubtless will, that he cannot master every study recommended, he will naturally first pursue those subjects which are obviously fundamental and less subject to change, in preference to those which are constantly shifting. He will give due consideration, too, to taking those courses for which there are great teachers available, realizing that there are many subjects that he can well teach himself rather than rely on a second-rate instructor.

Whatever studies he elects, he will endeavor, lawyer-like, to go so far as possible to the original sources rather than accept anyone's, even an expert's, opinions. He will struggle and inevitably learn to think for himself. He will aim to achieve not only exact knowledge but, even more important, correlated knowledge, leading to an understanding of the fundamentals of each subject he studies. He will strive for grasp and comprehension and hope that his efforts may be rewarded by insight.

As between the desire for knowledge and the necessity of training his faculties, he will place the emphasis on training. Knowledge inevitably comes to the trained mind. And he will realize that the test of both knowledge and training will ultimately be his ability to put them to the use of the community in which he lives. The challenge to his imaginaion was perfectly phrased three and a half centuries ago by one of the great romantic figures of history: "To what purpose," said Sir Philip Sidney, "should our thoughts be directed to various kinds of knowledge, unless room be afforded for putting it in practice, so that public advantage may be the result?"

Studying Law

Having successfully surmounted all the hurdles in being accepted at a law school in this highly competitive age, the student has the capacity to succeed at the school he attends. Many students, however, spend their first semester, or first year, struggling to determine exactly what the study of law is all about. Law school presents an inherently different type of challenge than college, and the differences between an undergraduate education and a legal education have become even more accentuated with the increasingly open-ended nature of academic requirements at many colleges. The transition from college to law school can therefore, often unexpectedly, be a difficult one.

During this inevitable period of adaptation to the law school world, it is all too easy to get off on the wrong track and never realize it until first semester exams are approaching, or over. It is ironic that during the very period when the first-year student is attempting to discover the correct approach to the study of law, the academic record he achieves and the mastery over the courses he attains can have ᐟ critical impact, if not the most important impact, on his early legal career. The period when the student is most likely to be overwhelmed or mystified by the law school experience is also the period when success in law school is most important.

If the student wishes to secure a law-related summer job after the first year, first-semester grades can be a central consideration. Students seeking a summer position after their second year of law school go through the interviewing process during the autumn of their second year, and again must depend on their first-year grades. Because law firms often like to see how a student works during a period of summer employment before deciding whether to hire him as an associate after graduation, a summer job with the law firm or type of law firm the student wishes later to join can be an important prelude to a legal career.

First-year grades are customarily the exclusive means of determining who will serve on the law school's law review, which in turn can be a major factor in determining who will be offered the most attractive jobs upon graduation. Of equal importance, it is the traditional first-year courses—contracts, criminal law, evidence, property, and torts—which will be the building blocks of many other law school courses and which almost all states now emphasize on their bar examinations; thus, the necessity of a thorough mastery of first-year material is obvious. Finally, as grades are the only type of information a law student receives about academic performance, they can have a marked effect on the student's attitude toward law school and his own legal abilities, and so, on future performance.

Recognizing the importance of the student's first-year success, there should be no mystery about how to apply oneself immediately to the particular demands of law school. Yet it is the rare student who enters law school with the knowledge of what a legal education requires and the rare professor who will take time to cast any light on the proper techniques of studying law. Indeed, law professors often seem to consider the tribulations of the first-year student a necessary initiation rite, although it is difficult to justify the potentially high costs of the initation dues in relation to what the student gains from the experience.

It is essential that the student knows what to expect from law school before commencing the study of law. By dispelling the clouds which have traditionally surrounded the student's introduction to the study of law, the student's transition into the law school environment will be eased and, rather than fighting his way through a maze of uncertainty and stress, he can immediately bring his talents to bear on the work at hand. While consistent hard work is the only foolproof formula for achieving the best record of which a student is capable, by understanding the general techniques of studying law—information that most law students eventually pick up on their own, but often not soon enough to benefit their first-year experience—the student from the first day of law school will better benefit from the effort and energy he pours into his work.

IN CLASS

For the prospective first-year student, what will occur in the classroom might loom as the most shrouded of law school mysteries. Without actions to remove the shrouds, it can remain a mystery, for what a particular course requires, let alone what to expect from the class, is information the student must often determine alone.

An opening passage from the novel *The Paper Chase*, by John Jay Osborn, Jr., contains a classic depiction of the first-year law student's first-day fears:

Most of the first year students, in anticipation of their first class at the Harvard Law School, were already seated as Professor Kingsfield, at exactly five minutes past nine,

walked purposefully through the little door behind the
lecture platform. He put his books and notes down on the
wooden lectern and pulled out the seating chart. One
hundred and fifty names and numbers: the guide to the
assigned classroom seats. He put the chart on the lectern,
unbuttoned his coat, exposing the gold chain across his
vest, and gripped the smooth sides of the stand, feeling
for the indentations he had worn into the wood. He did
not allow his eyes to meet those of any student—his face
had a distant look similar to the ones in the thirty or so
large gilt-framed portraits of judges and lawyers that hung
around the room. . . .

At exactly ten past nine, Professor Kingsfield picked a
name from the seating chart. The name came from the left
side of the classroom. Professor Kingsfield looked off to
the right, his eyes following one of the curving benches to
where it ended by the window.

Without turning, he said crisply, "Mr. Hart, will you
recite the facts of *Hawkins* versus *McGee?*"

When Hart, seat 259, heard his name, he froze. Caught
unprepared, he simply stopped functioning. Then he felt
his heart beat faster than he could ever remember its
beating and his palms and arms break out in sweat.

Professor Kingsfield rotated slowly until he was staring
down at Hart. The rest of the class followed Kingsfield's
eyes.

"I have got your name right?" Kingsfield asked. "You
are Mr. Hart?" He spoke evenly, filling every inch of the
hall.

A barely audible voice floated back: "Yes, my name is
Hart."

"Mr. Hart, you're not speaking loud enough. Will you
speak up?"

Hart repeated the sentence, no louder than before. He
tried to speak loudly, tried to force the air out of his lungs
with a deep push, tried to make his words come out with
conviction. He could feel his face whitening, his lower lip
beat against his upper. He couldn't speak louder.

"Mr. Hart, will you stand?"

After some difficulty, Hart found, to his amazement, he was on his feet.

"Now, Mr. Hart, will you give us the case?"

Hart had his book open to the case: he had been informed by the student next to him that a notice on the bulletin board listed *Hawkins* v. *McGee* as part of the first day's assignment in contracts. But Hart had not known about the bulletin board. Like most of the students, he had assumed that the first lecture would be an introduction.

His voice floated across the classroom: "I . . . I haven't read the case. I only found out about it just now."

Kingsfield walked to the edge of the platform.

"Mr. Hart, I will myself give you the facts of the case. *Hawkins* versus *McGee* is a case in contract law, the subject of our study. A boy burned his hand by touching an electric wire. A doctor who wanted to experiment in skin grafting asked to operate on the hand, guaranteeing that he would restore the hand 'one hundred percent.' Unfortunately, the operation failed to produce a healthy hand. Instead, it produced a hairy hand. A hand not only burned, but covered with dense matted hair.

"Now, Mr. Hart, what sort of damages do you think the doctor should pay?"

Hart reached into his memory for any recollections of doctors. There were squeaks from the seats as members of the class adjusted their positions. Hart tried to remember the summation he had just heard, tried to think about it in a logical sequence. But all his mental energy had been expended in pushing back shock waves from the realization that, though Kingsfield had appeared to be staring at a boy on the other side of the room, he had in fact called out the name Hart. And there was the constant strain of trying to maintain his balance because the lecture hall sloped toward the podium at the center, making him afraid that if he fainted he would fall on the student in front of him.

Hart said nothing.

"As you remember, Mr. Hart, this was a case involving a doctor who promised to restore an injured hand."

That brought it back. Hart found that if he focused on Kingsfield's face, he could imagine there was no one else in the room. A soft haze formed around the face. Hart's eyes were watering, but he could speak.

"There was a promise to fix the hand back the way it was before," Hart said.

Kingsfield interrupted: "And what in fact was the result of the operation?"

"The hand was much worse than when it was just burned. . . ."

"So the man got less than he was promised, even less than he had when the operation started?"

Kingsfield wasn't looking at Hart now. He had his hands folded across his chest. He faced out, catching as many of the class's glances as he could.

"Now, Mr. Hart," Kingsfield said, "how should the court measure the damages?"

"The difference between what he was promised, a new hand, and what he got, a worse hand?" Hart asked.

Kingsfield stared off to the right, picked a name from the seating chart.

"Mr. Pruit, perhaps you can tell the class if we should give the boy the difference between what he was promised and what he got, as Mr. Hart suggests, or the difference between what he got, and what he had."

Hart fell back into his seat. He blinked, trying to erase the image of Kingsfield suspended in his mind. He couldn't. The lined white skin, the thin rusty lips grew like a balloon until the image seemed to actually press against his face, shutting off everything else in the classroom.

Hart blinked again, felt for his pen and tried to focus on his clean paper. His hand shook, squiggling a random line. Across the room, a terrified, astonished boy with a beard and wire-rimmed glasses was slowly talking about the hairy hand.[1]

There are indeed professors who give assignments to be completed for their initial class meeting. To avoid the feeling of being behind on the first day of law school, it is prudent to find out at once where assignments are posted to determine what preliminary reading is required and what books must be purchased. In fact, it would well be worthwhile to arrive at law school a day or more before classes begin to have an informal opportunity to poke around the classrooms and law library before the halls are flooded with a mass of bewildered students.

If an initial reading assignment involves anything more than introductory material, it could indicate that the professor will be the type of teacher who plunges forward with machinelike efficiency to complete the concluding assignment on the last page of the syllabus by the final class of the semester; or it could be a terrorizing tactic to chill any notion the new students might have of their own legal brilliance. One Yale Law School professor was known to assign for his first class the case of *Fay* v. *Noia*[2]—a long federal *habeas corpus* case that even third-year students find difficult to decipher. Needless to add, after a frantic night of trying to make sense of *Fay*, the chilling effect was substantial.

The purpose behind this type of tactic is to illustrate dramatically to the class that law school is going to be a rigorous experience, even for the best of students. This is a fair warning, but the student should never let an initial assignment or any other terrorist tactic send him into a panic of despair about his ability to survive in law school. In this type of situation, as in many others during the first semester, the student's response could be compared to that of a swimmer caught out at sea: if he maintains his calm, breasting the waves, he is more likely to stay afloat and reach shore than if, overwhelmed by the enormity of the ocean and the limits of his swimming ability, he thrashes about, convinced that each breaker means doom. The student must maintain a certain tolerance for ambiguity and the unknown, while taking all reasonable steps to reduce the dimensions of the ambiguous and the unknown.

Lest it be thought that it is only the average student who could be so easily intimidated by a professor or who could so

easily encounter periods of self-doubt, hear the words of the
late Supreme Court Justice William O. Douglas, the quality of
whose mind was recognized as extraordinary even among
those who disagreed with his philosophies. In describing his
first class at Columbia Law School, Justice Douglas remembered his professor:

> Herman Oliphant, with his pointed nose and piercing
> eyes. . . . He had the skill of a brain surgeon in dissecting
> a legal problem. It was Oliphant who, on my very first day
> in Law School, embarrassed me before the class of 365
> students. He came into the room, placed his notes on the
> lectern, polished his glasses, and then paced the room—
> up one aisle, around in back, down the center aisle where
> he stopped at my row. I was on the aisle and, therefore,
> an easy victim. He asked my name, had me stand, and
> then asked, "Mr. Douglas, what is an estoppel?" My mind
> was blank. All I could say was, "I know it's not anything
> you find in the woods. Whether it is a legal principle or a
> disease, I haven't the least idea." I sat down, crushed and
> humiliated, certain that I was doomed as a lawyer.[3]

It should be noted that despite this painful classroom debacle,
Douglas survived to make the *Columbia Law Review* by the
end of his first year and to graduate from Columbia second in
his class. It might also be noted that despite this experience,
when Douglas himself upon graduation became a professor at
Columbia and later at Yale, he employed the same hard-bitten
techniques associated with the Socratic method, admitting later that "I tended to treat the class as the lion tamer in the
circus treats his wards."[4] Perhaps in just such a fashion are law
school traditions passed on in perpetuity.

There will be as many different styles of conducting a class
as there are professors at a law school. One traditional approach which is customarily emphasized in first-year classes is
the famed Socratic method. The professor poses a question
and calls a student's name from the class roll. If the student's

answer is satisfactory, the professor may throw a second more specific or penetrating question to the student or may move on to a different student. Through this type of Socratic dialogue, a legal theory or the principles of a case will be developed. Other professors will combine the Socratic method with a more traditional lecture format, while still others will call on students simply to ensure that the class is staying awake. Some professors will closely follow the casebook, discussing and dissecting the assigned cases in detail. Others will assume that the cases have been read and understood and will immediately launch their discussions on a more theoretical level. There are professors whose lectures will readily fall into clear outline form; there are others whose presentation might make the student wonder whether he bought the correct casebook or is sitting in the proper class.

Often the full dimensions of a professor's style will only emerge in a gradual, period-by-period and week-by-week process, so that merely by attending class and observing the professor in action the student will not be able to adapt himself to the class as quickly as necessary. For instance, it may be that a professor is such a confusing speaker that whatever the student will learn must be derived from assigned and independent reading. Or, for exam purposes a professor might expect a class to recall very specific bits of information he presented. These are traits of which the student should be aware from the start of the semester. Given the diversity of teaching styles and the need to adjust one's preparation, at least to some extent, to a professor's individual approach, an immediate problem the law student faces is to learn something about his professor.

The best source of the necessary inside information is from upperclass students who have had the professor, and preferably who have had the same course from the professor. Whatever informantion is imparted should always at first be treated with some caution. What students consider an easy or hard course, or a good or poor professor, can vary significantly and care must be taken to determine from what basis the speaker is offering his opinions. A professor who delights his class with machine gun bursts of one-liner jokes and a casual attitude toward the course may, for instance, be liked by all, but the upperclass student might neglect to add that at the end of the semester all found themselves confused and uncertain about major areas of material covered in the course. The first-year budding barrister shouldn't hesitate to press in with his questions to try to elicit the unique characteristcs of the professor and the course and to determine what can be expected from the class and the exam. The student should seek a number of second- or third-year opinions about the same professor until a clear picture begins to develop.

Some law schools do a good job of soliciting student evaluations of professors at the end of each semester. These are then compiled and made available to the students in the law library or central administrative office. Depending on the specificity of the evaluation forms and the percentage of students responding, these compilations can provide a wealth of information based on student reaction to the professor and his course. If there is any administrative control over the compilation process, the student should be aware that he may or may not be getting a complete picture; steps could have been taken to clean up the compilations, especially the sections for open comments, so that no professor was mortally wounded. If the student does sense that there could be some negative factors lurking behind a particular professor's profile, it will be time, again, to seek out some students who can supply the candid details. Professors have been known to mend their ways from year to year, often in direct response to a hostile set of evaluations, so it is always possible that student opinion or evaluation information is already somewhat out of date.

A helpful source of objective information is the *Directory of Law Teachers*, published annually by the Association of American Law Schools. These volumes, which will be shelved in the law library, contain the vital statistics on every law professor in the United States, including academic background, career history, books published, and positions held. The *Directory* is useful not only in verifying student speculation about a professor's past, but also in determining a professor's areas of expertise and interest, and, incidentally, in discovering facts that might help a student in becoming personally acquainted with a professor.

Finally, if the student sought an opportunity to talk to a professor about a specific question concerning the class, the conversation could open up to the course in general, or at least give the student a glimpse of the professor's out-of-class personality. In such an informal setting the professor might even be willing to talk about another professor's course, although he could well be wary of making any critical comments or of revealing another professor's game strategy.

These types of sources should be mined by the first-year student within the first week or two of classes to gain general insight into each professor and his course with the aim of discovering the best approach to a particular class. And, parenthetically, after the first semester or first year when the selection of courses and professors is the student's responsibility, the same sources should again be worked to make intelligent selections.

It is said that a student, in designing a curriculum, should pick the professor and not the course. While if a student wishes to take securities regulation and only one professor teaches it, the student has little choice but to sign on and take whatever consequences befall, in many instances it is possible to be more selective and exercise preferences. Does he want a tax professor who concentrates on the practical lawyering skills of tax law, or a professor interested more in the theory of taxation? Would a course in which the professor focused on an economic analysis of a subject, or a class in which not a single piece of economic jargon was ever uttered be more comfortable? Is he looking for an easy course to pick up a couple of credits, or is he anxious for a rigorous exposure to a subject because of the relation of that subject to his career plans? Does he want a professor who demands a great deal of student participation or has he had enough Socratic interrogation in the first year to be ready for a more peaceful atmosphere?[5] All such factors which differentiate professors should go into the decision-making process involved in selecting a semester's courses. In this process, a professor's advice and opinions can be a most valuable source of information. The student can talk to the professor who will be offering the course to get an idea of what it will entail and to find out what type of person he is. And, he now might freely seek a professor's general counsel concerning what courses he should take and what, for instance, are the differences between Professor X's, Professor Y's, and Professor Z's constitutional law classes.

As strange as it may seem, in addition to finding out some basic information about one's professor, it is often immediately necessary, or helpful, for the first-year student to determine some basic facts about the subject of the course. There are professors who spend the first, or the first several, class periods developing an overview of their course in general terms: its subject matter, areas that will be covered and omitted, its special characteristics, and its place in the fabric of the law. But there are also professors who in the first class plunge their students right into deep water, such as old Professor Kingsfield in *The Paper Chase* who at once began firing away questions about the theory of recovery for the person whose hand turned hairy in the case of *Hawkins* v. *McGee*.[6] Again, such behavior can be an *in terrorem* tactic or simply indicative of a professor's lack of understanding of the informational needs of the student. In either case, the student should on his own take care that the forest is never lost for the trees. It would be entirely possible, for example, for a professor to go through a semester of a torts class without ever explaining what a tort is or, perhaps, without even using the work "tort." One torts professor at the University of Virginia School of Law posed the simple question. "What is a tort?" as the first question on his exam and received a most surprising and unexpected collection of answers.

To ascertain what ball park one is in and to gain a very general picture of what a course is all about, the student might look up its definition in *Black's Law Dictionary*, study the introductory material to the casebook and become familiar with its table of contents, or survey any other sources that might be available in the law library—such as the introductory pages of a legal treatise on the subject—that provide a thumbnail sketch of what a tort is, or the purposes of civil procedure, or the types of interests that fall under the heading of "property." As the semester progresses with an interminable flood of cases, the student should make every effort not to lose sight of how these specific cases fit into the general structure of the course.

As noted by author Scott Turow in his book *One L: An Inside Account of Life in the First Year at Harvard Law School*, the study of law in the United States has remained essentially the same throughout this century:

When Roscoe Pound, who eventually became the dean of Harvard Law School, entered as a first-year student in 1889, he was required to take courses in Torts, Criminal Law, Property, Contracts, and Common-Law Forms of Action, a nineteenth-century version of Civil Procedure. He mastered the law by reading cases; in class, his professors taught in the Socratic method. . . . [T]he resemblances between Dean Pound's first year and mine [in 1975] are striking. For nearly a century now, American lawyers have been bound together by the knowledge that they have all survived a similar initiation; it is something of a grand tradition.[7]

In colonial America, there were no requirements for admission to the practice of law and little, if any, formal legal education. Often practicing at the early colonial courts were men of limited abilities and unsavory reputations. Indeed, the lawyer was held in so little estimation that Gabriel Thomas, in his "Historical and Geographical Account of the Province and Country of Pensilvania and of West-New-Jersey in America," written at the close of the seventeenth century, thus assailed the professional class:

> Of Lawyers and Physicians I shall say nothing, because this Country is very Peaceable and Healthy: long may it so continue and never have occasion for the Tongue of the one, nor the Pen of the other, both equally destructive to Men's Estates and Lives; besides forsooth, they, Hangman like have a License to Murder and make Mischief.[8]

Even with the establishment of law schools, training for the bar remained—well into the nineteenth century—primarily through the apprentice system and self-directed reading. As Abraham Lincoln wrote in 1858, "the cheapest, quickest and best way" to become a lawyer was to "read Blackstone's *Commentaries*, Chitty's *Pleadings*, Greenleaf's *Evidence*, Story's *Equity* and Story's *Equity Pleadings*, get a license, and go into practice and still keep reading."[9]

The year 1870, when Christopher Columbus Langdell was named dean of the Harvard Law School, marked the beginning of the modern era of legal education. It was Langdell who developed what became known as the "scientific study of law," or the case method for teaching law. This new method involved the abandonment of textbooks which set forth legal principles and the introduction of casebooks, collections of reports of actual cases arranged to illustrate the development of legal principles.

Dean Langdell reasoned that the "law, considered as a science, consists of certain principles or doctrines. To have such a mastery of these as to be able to apply them with constant facility and certainty to the evertangled skein of human affairs, is what constitutes a true lawyer . . . and much the shortest and best, if not the only way of mastering the doctrine effectually is by studying the cases in which it is embodied."[10] To Langdell, it seemed "to be possible to take such a branch of the law as Contracts, for example, and, without exceeding comparatively moderate limits, to select, classify, and arrange all the cases which had contributed in any important degree to the growth, development and establishment of its essential doctrines."[11]

With the movement from textbooks to casebooks composed of appellate court opinions came also a change in the role of the law professor from that of a lecturer expounding the law to that of a Socratic guide, leading the students through a question-and-answer technique to their own personal discovery of the law. The Socratic method of teaching drew forth the law and its rationale from the student through discussion, instead of attempting to pour information into him by lectures or recitations from textbooks.

The response to Langdell's new method of legal education was explosive. "To most of the students, as well as to Langdell's colleagues, it was abomination."[12] "The students were bewildered; they cut Langdell's classes in droves; only a few remained to hear him out. Before the end of the first term, his course, it was said, had dwindled to seven devoted men. . . . The school's enrollment fell precipitously."[13]

Yet Langdell prevailed. His deanship lasted until 1895, during which time Harvard, in initiating this revolution in legal training, became the preeminent law school in the United States. And Langdell's case study—Socratic method of instruction was spread by his disciples to other law schools so that by the end of the century its establishment was secure.[14]

Although Langdell's revolutionary method of teaching and studying law soon became an institution at every law school, it

has always been subject to criticism and debate, both because of
the difficulties involved for the professor—"in the hands of a
genuine scholar, skilled in the Socratic method, the case
method is indubitably the best; in the hands of a mediocre man
it is the very worst of all possible modes of instruction"[15]—and
because of the difficulties involved for the student—"for a considerable period only the particularly quick or talented students
take part in the debate."[16] The Socratic method has been felt to
be particularly unsuited to the "great and important class of
men of average ability" which "exists and always will exist in the
profession. . . . These men must be trained as well as those of
superior power."[17] Thus, always balancing the benefits of the
use of the Socratic method of legal instruction have been the
costs of the method in terms of time and effort expended in
relation to the amount of material covered and the amount of
confusion that can be generated.

Nevertheless, since the time of Dean Langdell, the study of
appellate court opinions has become the predominant method
of instruction in all law schools. The case method is based
upon the examination of judicial opinions to draw out principles of law by induction and to introduce the student to the
science and art of legal analysis. A legal education is not so
much designed to give the student an extensive knowledge of
the law as it is designed to provide the student a foundation
and framework for the understanding and application of the
law. Judicial opinions, usually in edited form, make up the
bulk of a casebook and are the starting point of classroom
discussion.

A professor will plan to cover a certain amount of material
during a class period. He could either present this material
directly as in a college lecture course, or he could use the
Socratic method to make the presentation more of a dynamic
exchange between professor and class. In employing the Socratic method, the professor might pose relatively concrete
questions, as in asking for the facts of a particular case, the

issues involved, the holding of the case, and how the court reached such a holding; or, as is more often associated with the Socratic method, he might pose a hypothetical problem—a fact situation based on a case or line of cases, but with the critical facts or issues altered in varying degrees from those with which the student is familiar—and then ask a student how he would deal with the new case. By exploring a subject in this manner, the reach of the law and the principles behind it begin to emerge and focus.

The benefits of this system, if properly utilized, are an intense exposure to methods of legal reasoning and analysis and the development of an ability to quickly come to grips with legal problems. In calling on a student for the statement of the case, that is, the facts and most narrow holding of a case, the student begins to learn the difference between a lawyer's accurate and intensive reading of material and the average layman's style of dealing with the printed word. The student will begin to develop the power to analyze, compress, arrange, and reduce ideas to clear expression, both orally and in writing, and to separate the court's ruling from the less important language of the opinion. Similarly, the testing of a student's formulation of a holding by a series of hypothetical situations which push the formulation toward the realm of the absurd allows the students to perceive the boundaries and limits of a rule of law and how it may be expected to stand up under later events. And a professor's probing of how a case could have been presented or argued so that the court would have decided for the losing party focuses the student's attention on the type of problem a lawyer encounters—the persuasion of a court to reach a desired answer in a new case as yet undecided.

The use of the Socratic method—more specifically, the fear of hearing one's name resounding in a crowded classroom, appended to a question only partially understood, concerning material only vaguely recollected—can account for some of the tension first-year students experience during their initial months at law school. If it becomes obvious that a professor is hitting everv name on his class list in no special order, the constant realizatio.. that your name could be next can sometimes have more of a paralyzing than a motivating effect, with students wiping their moist palms as they try to anticipate what will be asked and what to answer, rather than following the course of the class as it unfolds. This is unfortunate, for it often inhibits proper note-taking and a full understanding of the class.

One remedy for this problem is to get into the habit of becoming a voluntary participant in the discussion. In addition to the formal calling of names, student participation can be a great help in making a class as lively and meaningful as possible. When the student feels he can make a contribution to the discussion, he should volunteer an answer, a comment, or a question (although with the latter, the student should be aware that the professor will probably turn around and ask, "And how would you answer that one, Mr. Smith?"). The experience of talking in class on one's own initiative can be a cure for the dreadful anticipation of the day when the student's name on the class list catches the professor's eye. Also, by continually seeking opportunities to participate, the student will ensure that he is carefully following the class. At the other extreme, it is entirely possible to say too much or to voluntee too frequently during a class period, and the student should retreat before the professor's, or the class's, boredom with his voice becomes obvious.

Lacking the courage to become a voluntary class participant, the student should merely accept the fact that his name is on the professor's list and that one fine day he will be called. If the student has kept up with the reading and has a basic understanding of the material the professor is covering, a minimally satisfactory response to any question will not be difficult.

It should always be kept in mind that the room does not really become as hushed at it seems when your name is called, that all eyes in the classroom do not focus on you, and that you are not going to be judged by your peers by the profundity, or lack thereof, of your answer. Quite the contrary. Most students will be so busy with their notes and attempting to follow the course of the discussion that the only fact they will be aware of is that the name called was not their own. Others will be so relieved that they were not called that they will collapse once again into a momentary stupor. In any event, understanding the fickleness of fate, the sympathies of the class will be with the student. And as there are few genuinely sadistic professors, the professor's aim will not be to try to demonstrate the student's ignorance or to ensnare him in the limitations of his logic, but rather as quickly as possible to advance the line of thought he wishes to develop. The student should therefore answer to the best of his ability and not worry about the long-range consequences of his answer, for there are none. Most members of the class will not even remember that a particular student was called during a period, and if they do, will be unable to recollect what type of answer he gave. And rarely does a professor include the extent, or content, of class participation in his formulation of the student's grade.

A correlation between a student's oral performance in class and his performance in law school (that is, on his exams) is difficult, if not impossible, to draw. Occasionally, the student who is regualarly brilliant in class will write an equally brilliant exam, but it would be difficult to predict these types of correlations. Felix Frankfurter, a consummate debater in college who graduated third highest in his college class, recalled many years later his first day at law school. "The first day I was there I had one of the most intense frights of my life. I looked about me. Everybody was taller." So intimidated was the new student that he did not speak up "at all during the first year." How few of his fellow students must have realized the extent of their reticent colleague's grasp of the law! Years later, one of his law professors would read to his first-year class a remarkably perceptive analysis of a case and then stun the students by

noting, "I have been reading to you, gentlemen, from the
first-year blue book of Felix Frankfurter of the class of 1906."[18]

Upon being called, the student should take an immediate
stab at an answer in whatever way he can, whether it be by
redefining the question, isolating an aspect of the question he
can handle, or offering an answer he believes settles the question. It often will be clear from the professor's question
whether he wants a general reaction to an issue or theory or
whether he is looking for a more specific piece of information.
"You are thinking great thoughts," famed Harvard Dean Er-
win Griswold would boom to his classes, "but what does the
statute say? What does the case say?" The student therefore
may or may not be able to depend on his notes or casebook as
a prompter, a circumstance that will dictate to some degree
how he prepares for a class. While the student might hope to
give a polished answer, under the pressures of the immediate
moment this is rarely possible. Any answer will therefore suffice, at least as a starting point, and the student should not
worry that what he has just said is not as articulate or as
insightful as that of which he is capable.

If the student doesn't understand the question, he could ask
for it to be repeated or rephrased, although it would be much
preferable to try to state specifically what he does not understand, a response which sometimes can be an answer in itself.
If he is unprepared, he should so state, although almost all
professors will mark this down on the roll and will be sure to
strike again. Giving this response will therefore only intensify
the pressures on the student during each succeeding class period. The best policy is to take a shot at the question, even if
not certain what answer the professor is looking for or what a
correct answer would be.

In addition to helping make a class more interesting, student
participation can be a most effective weapon in exerting a be-
nevolent control over the class. It may become evident that a
professor is a rapid-fire lecturer, spewing forth facts and the-

ories at a nonstop pace that makes meaningful note-taking a real burden. One property class at the New York University School of Law which was experiencing just such a professor chipped in to hire a court reporter for an hour to see if he could keep up. To no one's surprise, he couldn't. A class can sit and take this treatment, suffering collective finger cramps and severe intellectual indigestion, or it can fight back by raising a number of pertinent questions each period that will force the professor to slacken his pace or to explain the material more fully.

In other instances, it may not be clear exactly what the professor is trying to convey. The natural reaction in such a circumstance is for the student to assume that the fault lies with himself and that if he were brighter he would certainly understand as readily as everyone else in the room. However, it must always be kept in mind that teaching a law class is no easy matter. Justice William O. Douglas wrote in his autobiography about spending eight hours in preparation for each one-hour class, even after having taught at Columbia Law School and Yale Law School for several years.[19] To conduct a class at a high level takes a great deal of preparation or experience, or a combination of both. Obviously there will be classes for which a professor is less prepared than others, as well as a wide range of levels of ability among professors to communicate clearly to the majority of the class. The student can be quite certain that if he is having trouble understanding the points a professor is making, there are many others in the room who are experiencing the same troubles. It therefore benefits everyone if a student in such instances raises his hand and seeks to have a point clarified. Again, the more specific the student can be in stating what it is he doesn't understand, the better.

As has been stated, participation in class, which can create a certain amount of anxiety in students, has no serious long term after-effects. On the other hand, note-taking, which is the student's central in-class function, can have a most significant impact on the student's law school performance.

One of the casualties of the relaxation or modernization of secondary school and college requirements has been the ability to take notes. In a more traditional academic environment, the student served a long apprenticeship during which he could perfect his note-taking skills, for it often was the case that success in a course depended primarily on feeding back to a teacher on an exam exactly what the teacher had taught, the closer to a verbatim transcript the better. Now, with a premium being put on the ability to write papers or to speculate creatively on abstract exam questions, the ability to take notes is rapidly becoming a lost art. By the time the student arrives at law school, he is likely to be unaware of the value of a set of class notes or to be incapable of producing a valuable set.

What is done in class is not merely a review of what the student reads in his casebook. Not only is the professor likely to bring new material, or additional material, to his presentation of a subject, but on a startling number of occasions what the professor finds in a case or spins out from a case can be beyond the student's wildest imagination. Therefore, unless the student has a reliable photographic memory, he will find it necessary to record what goes on in each class in a written form that will be meaningful to him.

What follows are some suggestions on the mechanics of note-taking, although each student will develop on his own the exact method he finds most successful.

There are advantages in using a looseleaf notebook rather than a spiral notebook or legal pads. By the end of the semester, a notebook of class notes has become a priceless commodity to the student. If this body of knowledge is contained in a spiral notebook which must be brought back and forth to class each day, the student is risking the possibility that it will be lost, misplaced, or permanently borrowed, with all the consequential trauma that can place on a student at that time of year. Pages of notes taken on legal pads can easily tear off and again scatter to places unknown. But if the student has been taking his notes in a looseleaf notebook, at the end of each day these notes can be slipped out of his general notebook and put in individual looseleaf notebooks for each course, which can be kept safely in his room. He therefore will never have to carry an entire set of notes out into the cruel world. Also, the loose-leaf method will tend to preserve the notes from the everyday rips, tears, and coffee spills that can mangle a spiral notebook or legal pad by semester's end. And if a fellow student has missed a class and wants to borow the notes, it is a simple matter to slip the appropriate pages out of the looseleaf note-book, rather than handing over the entire set and worrying whether it will be ingested by a duplicating machine or held for ransom.

Because of the long-term value of class notes, they should be taken in pen rather than pencil, since pencil notes tend to smear or fade with handling and time. They should be written as legibly and as neatly as possible so that a week after the particular class they are not a mass of hieroglyphics that must be translated before being studied. And the student might want to consider starting each class with a fresh page and writing on only one side of the paper.

Of more importance than the methods of taking notes is what will be included in the notes. After a class period is over and has been followed by additional weeks of classes, the stu-dent's notes should be able to spark the main ideas that were presented as well as the supporting details to explain or clarify those ideas. While it is pointless to try to record every word a professor speaks, there is nothing more frustrating than re-turning to one's notes and discovering that, though legibly written in English, the words and sentences on a page are most decidedly cryptic. The student must therefore find for himself that point at which his notes will be neither unneces-sarily wordy nor too abbreviated.

Many students have found a standard outline form to be the most convenient framework in which to develop the notes of a class. If the student can fit the discussion of a class into outline form—with major headings, followed by subheadings, followed by specific supporting points, although with each heading and point perhaps including several sentences or a short paragraph rather than just words or brief phrases—it is likely that the student has intelligently followed the class and has a sound understanding of what went on during that hour. Notes in such a flexible outline style will be an easy form in which to digest the material.

While there is no substitute for one's own notes, at times class attendance might be impossible. On those occasions, the student should borrow a colleague's notes to copy or photocopy. This is an especially tricky business, for the first-year student cannot be certain how well his friends are following a course or how well they are incorporating what went on in class into their notes. If, after copying or studying the notes, he still doesn't have a solid grasp of what transpired during the class he missed, the student should borrow other students' notes until the class has come as fully into focus as if he had been there himself.

The secret to success in class—whether it be in the student's classroom participation or in his personal note-taking—is concentration. Unless a professor is one of those rare teachers who can regularly keep a class captivated with its full attention riveted on him, the student will find that, without a conscious effort to concentrate, his mind will begin to wander away from the subject being discussed. It is all too easy to lose focus on the matter at hand as a lawn mower hums on a playing field on a warm spring day, or as Friday afternoon approaches and the clock seems stuck at 2:50, or as the subject being discussed begins to seem, in the words of Oliver Wendell Holmes the elder, very much like sawdust without butter.

It would appear that all law students have had moments when their degree of concentration slipped. William Paterson, who served as attorney general of New Jersey after the Ameri-

can Revolution and as an associate justice of the United States
Supreme Court from 1793 until 1806, quite regularly com-
plained during his student days about his inability to concentrate on his legal studies. "Even resolving to apply closely to
[the law]," he judged to be "no inconsiderable conquest."[20]
And even the great John Marshall, Chief Justice of the United
States and the principal founder of the American system of
constitutional law, seemed to have had a hard time keeping his
mind on the lectures of his professors, ". . .for on the inside
cover and opposite page of the book on which he made notes
of . . . law lectures, we find in John Marshall's handwriting
the words, 'Miss Maria Ambler;' and again 'Miss M. Ambler;'
and still again, this time upside down, 'Miss M. Ambler—J.
Marshall;' and 'John Marshall, Miss Polly Am.;' and 'John,
Maria;' and 'John Marshall, Miss Maria;' and 'Molly Ambler;'
and below this once more 'Miss M. Ambler;' on the corner of
the page where the notes of the first lecture are recorded is
again inscribed in large, bold letters the magic word,
'Ambler.' "[21] And indeed, throughout the notebook, he occasionally scrawled "Polly Ambler," "Polly," "Miss Maria Ambler," or "Miss M. Ambler."[22] It would certainly seem that
when his professors were lecturing on the English common
law and decisions of the Privy Council, the future jurist's
thoughts were drifting around the woman he soon was to
marry.

Often, it will only be in reviewing his classroom notes and
finding a puzzling gap in the professor's presentation, or in
trying to reconstruct what occurred in a class period and discovering that the hour was somewhat of a blank, that the
student will even realize that he was not fully following the
period's discussion. It is only through a very conscious effort of
forcing the mind to concentrate that the student may ensure
that he derives the full benefit from each class and that he will
not find himself, at some not too distant date, attempting to
learn material for the first time that was discussed while he

was daydreaming. Becoming a classroom participant or devoting oneself to preparing a valuable set of notes are the easiest ways to guarantee that one's concentration will remain at a high level throughout each class period.

There is a story told of a philosophy professor at Yale who taught an upperclass course which one semester was taken by only one student. The professor strode into the lecture hall at the beginning of each class, delivered his discourse, and departed, without once, throughout the entire semester, acknowledging the personal presence of his only auditor.

Happily, the days when any interaction between students and professors was confined to the classroom, if there was indeed any interaction there, are disappearing in colleges and universities as well as in law schools. It is common practice for students who have questions to talk to the professor immediately after the class period ends. Most professors are willing to field questions for a good ten minutes after class or longer if their schedule permits. If the student wants to talk to the professor on an individual basis, it is entirely appropriate to stop by his office. Many professors follow an open-door policy and encourage, or at least do not discourage, such out-of-class contact.

In addition to clarifying points the student did not understand in class, or seeking general guidance concerning a course or his law school work, there are several secondary benefits related to getting to know a professor. First, no matter how hard-boiled or heartless a professor might seem in class, it is often a pleasant surprise to see his more human characteristics emerge when he is "off stage" in his office. This in itself can help the student better understand a professor's classroom strategy. Typical is attorney Melvin Belli's remembrance of one of his professors at law school.

Kidd intimidated the entire class. When he stalked into the classroom, you could hear everyone sucking in his breath . . . "There is an uprising and the President has declared martial law. Does the writ of habeas corpus still apply? Belli?"

"Yyy-yes," I'd stammer.

Then he would stare at me for a moment with the bluest, coldest eyes I had ever seen, throw down the eyeshade he invariably wore on top of the few white hairs he had on his head and cry: "You numbskull. You're all numbskulls. It's a crime your parents are keeping you in school."

Yet, Belli noted, "despite Captain Kidd's behavior in class, he was the kindest, most approachable guy on the faculty when you went to him in his office."[23]

Second, most professors are very willing to help the student with whatever problems or quesions he might have about a particular course or about his law school experience and future legal plans, and are, of course, a source of valuable insight and advice on such matters. Third, considering the size of most law school classes, it is impossible for the professor to get to know the students on an individual basis, let alone even learn their names. Since in applying for summer jobs or a position after graduation a faculty recommendation is often required or requested, such student contact with the professor outside of class can be a useful means, and often the only means, for the professor to gain more than a superficial acquaintance with the student. Finally, the professor is probably just as eager to get to know something about the members of his class as the students are to learn something about the professor. Appearances to the contrary notwithstanding, it is hard to believe a professor would really want his students to dislike him. Most are anxious to hear of student reaction to their courses, to know what areas the students find difficult, to get to know some of those one hundred and thirty-two people who stare at them each day with sullen hostility or boredom or hopeless incomprehension. For all of these reasons, the student should not be hesitant in consulting the professor outside of class, while at the same time being careful not to become a burden on his time.

STUDYING

The classroom can be the arena where much of the drama and excitement of a legal education is enacted, but what takes place in class is not the major part of the law student's education. A general rule of thumb is that the student should work at least two hours on a course for every hour spent in class. If the student is taking five courses, each of which meets three hours a week, he will spend fifteen hours in class, and, following the general rule, about thirty hours preparing for the classes and studying the courses—a total of forty-five hours a week. Working six days a week, this averages out to seven and a half hours of work each day. With experience, the student will be able to determine how much time he must spend, or wants to spend, on each course; but because of the importance of one's first-year record, coupled with one's inability at this stage to gauge precisely how much time must be devoted to the law, it is better to err on the side of spending too much time on each subject than too little.

The student should reconcile himself to spending almost all of his time during the first semester of law school studying law. He will quickly discover the truth in such ancient saws as "The Law is a jealous mistress" and "Lady Law must lie alone." As Justice Joseph Story wrote in the early nineteenth century, "I will not say with Lord Hale that 'The Law will admit of no rival,' but I will say that it is a jealous mistress, and requires a long and constant courtship. It is not to be won by trifling favors, but by lavish homage,"[24] And, as Melvin Belli discovered a century later when he was a law student: "I started really to study. I don't know whether I was struck with the learning lightning then or whether I started to study because it was the custom for students to put as many hours into the law books as they could until they dropped. For the three years at Boalt Hall [University of California] I studied from eight in the morning until twelve at night, including Saturday and Sunday, Thanksgiving, New Year's, Christmas, and through the summer vacation."[25] As William Blackstone noted, "It is true that this profession, like all others, demands of those who would succeed in it an earnest and entire devotion."[26]

In addition to the necessity of understanding each assignment covered in the casebook and classroom so that every succeeding block of material is comprehensible and in perspective, there are two primary goals of studying which require different approaches. The immediate goal is to be familiar with the material to a sufficient degree so that what takes place in the classroom will be meaningful and so that the student is prepared to be a participant, whether voluntary or involuntary. The second goal is to master the material for the purposes of the semester exams, and, more generally, to make the material a permanent part of one's working knowledge of the law.

To be adequately prepared for class, the student will want to be specifically familiar with the details of the assigned materials. Without attempting to memorize bits of information, he will want to be conversant with the peculiarities of the cases, the names of the parties, and the specific considerations determinative of the resolution of the issues. It is therefore often of little value to read too far ahead in a casebook or to prepare an assignment too far before the class will meet, for in the intervening days filled with other cases and classes, the particular facts and principles contained in the assignment will begin to dim and blur. Rather, the student should plan his schedule so that he can prepare an assignment a day or two before the class in which it will be discussed. Because of the limited consequences of one's classroom performance and because the specific details of each and every case need not be retained for the exams, it is a waste of time to study intensely a block of material at this point with the hope of being able to answer any question a professor might pose in class. What the student recalls from a careful recent reading will be sufficient for performing adequately in class and for gaining the greatest value from a class.

To prepare for class, the student should first preview the assigned material, taking about five minutes to skim through the pages noting the headings, the number and length of the cases involved, and the nature of any supplemental material. It can also be of value to examine the table of contents to see just where the cases fit into the overall subject area. These few minutes devoted to gaining an overview of the assignment will be well spent, for if the student begins studying without any idea of the relation of the material to what went before and what will come after, he will probably read the bulk of an assignment before its special relevance becomes clear.

The assignment can then be attacked. Cases cannot be read in the same way as short stories. The student should not be alarmed that his reading speed declines remarkably while working through a series of cases, for learning the language of the law is almost equivalent to learning a foreign language.

Perhaps the steepest hurdle all beginning law students will first encounter is the strange new world of legal language. Lawyers and judges seem to have a "peculiar cant and jargon of their own, that no other mortal can understand," Gulliver said of the people he met in his travels. Lawyers have ignored such Swiftian barbs for centuries, and have continued the practice of their mysterious science, inaccessible to the uninitiated.

Yale University law professor Fred Rodell described the language of the law as "almost deliberately designed to confuse and muddle the ideas it purports to convey. No segment of the English language in use today is so muddy, so confusing, so hard to pin down to its supposed meaning as the language of the law. It ranges only from the ambiguous to the completely incomprehensible."[27] And Berkeley Law Dean Sanford Kadish calls lawyers masters of "a mysterious art form to which the layman is not privy, with mumbo jumbo going on."[28] Indeed, in light of the impenetrable language of the law, some cynics have suggested that lawyers write laws in undecipherable language to guarantee employment for future generations of lawyers, who will be the only people capable of understanding them.

There is a small but growing national movement of consumers and institutions rebelling against legalese. In 1975, giant Citibank pioneered the move to write consumer loans, mortgages and bank card contracts in easily understandable, everyday English. A New York law passed in 1977 ordered all consumer contracts to be written in understandable language. And President Carter tried to reform the murky language of federal regulations. But students are still indoctrinated in legalese from their first day in law school. Wrote Scott Turow in *One L:*

It's obvious, in looking back, that one of the things which made me feel most at sea initially was the fact that I barely understood much of what I was reading or learning. Before we'd left for the East, one California lawyer-friend advised me to remember that in many ways a legal education was just the learning of a second language. In those first days, I saw exactly what he meant. What we were going through seemed like a kind of Berlitz assault in "Legal," a language which I didn't speak and in which I was being forced to read and think sixteen hours a day. Of course Legal bore some relation to English—it was more a dialect than a second tongue—but it was very peculiar. It was full of impossible French and Latin terms—*assize, assumpsit, demurrer, quare, clausum fregit,* thousands more. . . .

And beyond new words employed in novel ways, there was a style of written argument with which we had to become familiar. In reading cases, I soon discovered that most judges and lawyers did not like to sound like ordinary people. . . . They wanted their opinions to seem the work of the law, rather than of any individual. To make their writing less personal and more impressive, they resorted to all kinds of devices, "whences" and "heretofores," roundabout phrasings, sentences of interminable length.

This is from *Batsakis* v. *Demotsis*, the first case we read in *Civil Procedure:*

". . .*under the circumstances alleged in Paragraph II of this answer, the consideration upon which said written instrument sued upon by plaintiff herein is founded is wanting and has failed to the extent of $1975.00, and defendant pleads specially under the verification hereinafter made and want the failure of consideration stated, and now tenders, as defendant has heretofore tendered to plaintiff, $25.00. . .*"

To wade through stuff like that took time—astonishing amounts of time. Before I'd started school, I could not believe that reading a few cases every day in each course could possibly absorb more than a couple of hours. In the first week, none of the cases was longer than two or three pages, but between the drawing of case briefs and my frequent detours to the dictionary, I did not have a moment to spare.[29]

The first-year student must fight the temptation to gloss over the new words or phrases he does not understand, for without learning their meaning and perceiving how they are used in the context of a case, the student will fall into a false sense of complacency about his understanding of an assignment. Much of his time will be spent with a law dictionary as he works his way carefully through an assignment. Justice Hugo Black decided to teach his son something about the law before he started law school. He gave him a copy of Holmes's *Common Law* and told him to read a section and then the two of them would discuss it.

The first night after dinner, Justice Black took the book from his son and asked him what part he had read. His son remembered that evening:

> I showed him. Right off he said, "What is a tort?"
> "I don't know."
> "Hmm," he said. "What is a conversion?"
> "Conversion is when you change from one thing to another."
> He closed the book and threw it at me.
> "Good Lord, it's worse than I thought. You're either too lazy to use the dictionary or you don't know how. You're not ready to discuss anything. Don't ever come in here again telling me you've read something when you don't even know what key words mean. Now spend the rest of the night learning the words you passed over that might as well be ink spots for all they mean to you.[30]

In addition to the time necessary for learning a new vocabulary and a new language, the student's reading speed will also suffer as he makes annotations in the margins and highlights pertinent sections of the cases as he proceeds. Such study aids can be a useful means of noting important points for easy retrieval in class or when reviewing the case, and, again, can help ensure that the student is reading the cases critically. The student should take care that he marks only the most relevant sections of an opinion, for it is of little value to have almost every sentence underlined; this usually indicates that the student was not reading the opinion thoughtfully.

The student should brief each case immediately after it has been read. Briefing not only provides an opportunity to study and review the case to see if it was fully understood, but also provides a written summary to refresh the student's recollection of the case during class or months later when he is studying for his exam.

A standard form of briefing is as follows:

The name of the case is written at the top of a page along with the court which decided it and the year it was decided.

Underneath, the bare, essential facts of the case are stated. Only those facts which the student finds absolutely critical to understanding the decision should be summarized. The facts of almost any case can usually be stated in several sentences or a short paragraph. Abbreviations, such as "p" for plaintiff and "d" for defendant, should be used to reduce further the complexities of the facts of the case to their starkest form.

The issues involved in the case are stated next. What was the issue with which the court was faced, given the facts of the case? What was it attempting to determine? There may be several issues, but one should stand out as most important to the case and to the immediate court material or else the case would not be in the casebook in this particular spot or be read at this particular time. The issue should be stated in the form of a one-sentence question, often beginning with the word "whether": whether there is an implied warranty in a lease for the quiet enjoyment of the leased premises; whether a widow convicted of manslaughter in connection with the death of her husband may inherit from his estate; whether there are any standards to be applied in determining if specific payments are income or gifts.

The holding of the case follows. This should be a one-sentence statement that answers the question posed by the issue. What has the court decided? What does the case stand for? If the student can isolate and extract the core issue and the core holding of a case—a skill he will acquire through repeated briefings—he can be confident that he has a sound, basic understanding of the case.

The reasoning by which the court arrived at the decision can then be summarized. On what legal, practical, theoretical, precedential, or policy grounds did the court base its opinion? The student should not attempt to recapture the full complexities of the court's reasoning, but should merely summarize each point he believes was an important basis in reaching the decision.

When a decision includes a concurring or dissenting opinion, the reasoning of these minority opinions can be briefly stated in a short paragraph or as a series of points. Although minority opinions do not represent the settled "law" of the case, they often can help throw light on the reasoning of the majority or illustrate the questionable or debatable aspects of the majority's rationale.

A complete brief of almost any case can fit on one side of a page of paper. If a student's briefs tend to run substantially longer, it is possible that he is merely taking notes on the case rather than wrestling with the case in a critical manner. In studying an area of law, there are great advantages to be derived from having stripped a case to its essential framework and from having isolated its meaning in one's own words.

As soon after a class meets as is possible, the student should reread his class notes, underscoring those points which upon reflection were most important, and amplifying any sections he recorded incompletely. Similarly, he may now return to his briefs to mark the points the professor stressed or to add material the professor found important that the student on his first reading did not. The student should write down any questions he still has concerning the material and attempt to answer the questions as soon as possible, either through outside reading or through talking with his professor or colleagues.

A lawyer's mind has been compared to a bathtub filled up with legal knowledge in regard to each new problem he handles and then drained to ready it for the next case. This analogy is less accurate in relation to the law student's mind; though much of the specific information concerning cases can be drained or allowed to atrophy without consequence, at a minimum a core of principles concerning each course must be retained at least through the examination period.

After the material for a class has been read and briefed, the class has met and the material has been discussed, and the student has reviewed and clarified his briefs and class notes, he will know more about that discrete area of law than he ever will unless he chances to encounter the area again in his professional career. His study of the material, however, is not complete. The most important aspect of his study remains. It is at this time—the day the class has met or certainly within the week—that the student must distill his knowledge of the assignment to its pith and commit it to his outline of the course. It is the boiling away of the material to its essence—like boiling gallons of maple sap to produce a quart of maple syrup—that is the heart of the intellectual process of studying law. Because the preparation of an outline is the most important single avenue to success in law school, it will be treated separately later in this section.

It should be no secret that just as in college the student found there were review notes or "trots" available for almost every conceivable work of literature, so there are prepared notes for almost every legal subject and every casebook in current use. These are called by various names: case digests, law summaries, outlines, or legal outlines. Some are published commercially by companies specializing in the outline business. They can include briefs of every case in a casebook or can be in the form of an outline of the legal subject such as the student would prepare for each of his courses. Others are prepared for sale by students of the law school and therefore are geared even more closely to a particular professor's course, sometimes even capturing for posterity the exact sentences and hypotheticals the professor uses year after year. Both commercial and student outlines will be for sale in the law school bookstore, and the commercial companies as well as the student authors usually manage to have a generous supply of advertisements posted at various strategic spots in the law school.

For a student who is having difficulty with a course, the

existence of such aids will seem like an answer to all his prayers. Cautioning him against their use would be as easy as warning a shipwrecked, sun-beaten sailor not to drink salt water. Nevertheless, the dangers involved with their use must be very clearly recognized.

There is no guarantee that these outlines or summaries are accurate; the student could therefore get an incorrect picture of the law. There is no guarantee that they are complete; what an outline reports about a case, what a student might have gotten out of it by reading it himself, and what the professor draws out of it can vary dramatically. There is no guarantee that they are up-to-date; some professors take a special delight in annually altering their material to stay one jump ahead of the professional outliners.

But perhaps most dangerous of all is the ease with which these prepared materials can become a crutch which inhibits or stunts the student's legal growth. No matter what his intention in buying an outline—as a supplement to or substitute for the study of assigned materials—the temptation to depend on them exclusively can become irresistible when work is piling up, when reading assignments are getting longer, when the student feels that the law is indeed becoming a very jealous mistress.

There are some students who get to the point where they bring these outlines to class, take notes in them only to fill in an occasional gap, and don't bother their casebooks again for the rest of the semester. Some students who follow this practice come out unscathed after exams, although by dealing only with a skeleton of a subject they will have missed much of the sinew and blood that make the law a part of life itself.

But often the student who feels he needs the type of help he expects the outlines to provide will suffer the most from relying on them. If he actually attempts to use them in conjunction with his casebook and notes, he will probably discover that he is spending more time trying to see how the outline fits

the material than he would in working through the material on
his own. And if he becomes dependent on them, he will be
bypassing the intellectual process which most people must experience to be able to learn a legal subject in anything more
than a superficial sense. It can become too easy to consider the
material in an outline as a body of concrete knowledge simply
to be memorized, without understanding the dynamic tensions
and tugs behind the material—which is what the study of law
is all about. To depend on commercial outlines in lieu of reading the cases and preparing one's own outlines is to miss the
heart of the learning experience of law school and to be only
temporarily aware of a large body of law which properly should
be a part of one's permanent equipment. It is also to run the
substantial risk of finding oneself completely unable to cope
with the problems on an exam, either because the exam covers
material which the outline neglected, or because the student
has not gained a facility for working with or thinking about a
particular subject.

The first-year student would therefore be well advised to
follow the ancient doctrine of *caveat emptor* before submitting
to the siren song of a commercially packaged route to law
school success.

There can of course be times when despite a student's best
efforts a case remains enigmatic or an area of law confusing. In
such instances the student should move outside his casebook
and classes to approach the material from a different angle.
The possibilities for outside reading in a particular field are
almost without limit as a quick survey of a law library will
reveal, but given the constraints on the student's time there
are two sources which can be turned to immediately for instant
clarification.

If the student is having difficulty with a case, he should
look the case up in the state or federal reports containing it.
The opinion will be preceded by headnotes which summarize
the facts of the case and include abstracts of the issues and

the holdings of the case classified by subject. An examination of the headnotes will usually be enough to reveal all the keys to the case and make a second reading of the casebook material more meaningful.

If the student is puzzled by an area of the law, the best source of enlightenment is a hornbook or legal treatise on the subject of the course in question. These textbooks of one or more volumes differ from casebooks in that they are like encyclopedias and set out the law of a subject rather than present primary materials of actual judicial opinions. Some, like *Prosser on Torts* and *Corbin on Contracts*, are well-respected authorities which are often cited by courts, and frequently a professor will recommend a hornbook as supplemental reading. Through the use of the table of contents, table of cases, or index, the student will instantly be able to find the pages relevant to the area of a legal subject he is studying and will find the law set out as clearly there as anywhere.

As with prepared briefs or outlines, study groups are a law school institution which the student should fully understand before concluding that they are a shortcut system to success in law school. A study group is a group of students, usually about five or six and rarely more than ten, who band together for mutual aid and support. The students, all taking the same courses from the same professors, gather at specified intervals to review the work covered in each class, to talk out problems with the classes, and to discuss exam strategies. Usually the students divide up the courses among themselves with each member of the study group becoming a specialist in one of the courses. That student has the responsibility to do any extra research needed to answer questions the other members of the group might have, and the specialist prepares the outline for that course. This outline is then duplicated and each member of the group receives a copy before the exam.

Study groups can provide a convenient forum for the discussion of the law, which can be an important part of the student's legal education and a means of gaining a working knowledge of different legal subjects. By pooling their knowledge, each student receives the benefit of a range of insights into the mechanical and substantive aspects of a course. And the use of the specialist system can cut down on the time the student must devote to each class.

But there can also be serious limitations to the study-group method of studying law. A study group will be no better than the students who comprise it. Unless the students knew each other before coming to law school, they will have little idea of the intellectual capabilities of their associates. There is therefore always the possibility that a group could exemplify the proverbial dangers of the blind leading the blind, or resemble the merchant convoys crossing the Atlantic in the days of World War II, with the convoy never able to move faster than the slowest ship. In such instances, the student might well be better off on his own. Also, there is the possibility that when it comes time to distribute the outlines, one or more of the outlines might prove to be disappointing or inadequate or one student might prove to be the type of person who simply cannot complete a project to meet a deadline. If the group has been depending on each of the outlines for exam preparation, the fortunes of the whole group could be endangered by such eventualities. Of course, this type of disaster could be avoided by distributing the outlines piecemeal throughout the semester. Even so, there are those study-group members who will find that they do superbly on the exam in the subject for which they were the specialist, but perform less well on the other exams. Here again, as with the use of prepared outlines, if the student bypasses too much of the personal intellectual process of coming to grips with each course—a process which many students find calls for the preparation of their own outlines—he may discover too late that he has not developed the ability to work with a subject to the degree called for by an examination.

THE OUTLINE

The outline the student prepares for each course is the most important key to law school success.

An outline is the distillation of the student's case briefs, casebook notes, and class notes. It would seem that the preparation of such an outline should be a simple matter; this would perhaps be so if the professor presented his material with crystal clarity and if the casebook were laid out in an easily digestible form. More often than not, however, in class and in preparing casebooks, professors intentionally or unintentionally play a game which students have called, in their more charitable moments, "hide the ball." Often it is not the professor's purpose to set out the material so plainly that all the student need do is memorize it and repeat it on his exam to earn a good grade. Instead, it is the student's responsibility to dig out the law and the rationale behind it from an amorphous mass of material. It is the student's job to separate the wheat of relevance from the classroom chaff, to spot the issues that are being raised, to identify the solutions that are suggested, and to understand what theories and policies support the solutions. In the same respect, casebook editors do not usually follow a case with a statement on the holding of the case or the law it settled. It is the student's business to pry these crystals from the matrix of the cases and to comprehend the reasoning by which a court arrived at a decision.

To a certain extent, this "hide the ball" teaching method is a very accurate reflection of the law itself. Always in a state of flux and change, the law does not offer as much certainty and predictability as the layman might expect. The practice of law is not a process of looking up hard-and-fast rules to solve any given problem. A law professor at Indiana University annually offers a twenty-dollar prize to the student who can present him with a "simple legal problem." Many have confidently come up with seemingly straightforward problems, such as "when is a person legally dead" or "when has a will be attested to by three witnesses," only to have the professor draw out all the ambiguities inherent in the problems that have led to a confused and conflicting mass of litigation. The study of law can therefore be a fluid enterprise with the student himself the only source of whatever certainty or conclusions might be drawn from the mass of material presented by his professor and casebook. He must seek and find the ball in the professor's game of "hide the ball," whether the ball be considered the rules of law, the black-letter law, the important points contained in a block of material, or the conclusions to be drawn from the material.

Sometimes this game can be carried to such an extent— either because of the professor's conscious effort to hide the ball or because of his inability to communicate with clarity— that the student is not only unaware of where the ball is hidden; he is not even aware of what kind of ball he is looking for. Wrote the eminent Professor Grant Gilmore in a review discussing the teaching of law:

> We shy off from organizing our material into a coherent whole on the excuse that to do so would be spoonfeeding. At best, we give our students a series of unrelated flashes of brilliance; at worst, nothing.
>
> I was once a law student myself and, if the record is to be believed, a moderately good one. Yet, there was hardly a course through the entire six terms whose principle of organization was apparent to me while I was taking the course or after I had finished it. Each new case or group of cases was a surprise package whose relationship to what went before and came after was and remained an impenetrable mystery. The quantity and the quality of the rabbits which my instructors produced from empty hats filled me with awe and occasionally with reverence, but the production did not, I think, substantially contribute to my education.[31]

The student's development of an outline is therefore not merely an act of summarizing or synthesizing. It is a process of creative intelligence by which he must force the material of a course into a coherent, organized, and meaningful form.

The greater the care he has expended on his briefs and class notes, the easier outlining will be. And the more regularly he keeps his outline current, the less of a burden it will be. If the student lets several weeks elapse before organizing the material into an outline, he not only will be faced with the unpleasant prospect of devoting a large block of time to the intense and draining task of mastering a major section of material, but he also will have lost some of the value of each succeeding class by not having the material that went before in proper perspective. It is therefore recommended that the student prepare a running outline, kept up-to-date after every class or at the very least on a week-to-week basis. An outline for each course should be begun the first week of the first semester.

Every effort should be made to reduce all the learning from one class period's assignment to a single side of a single page of an outline. This will not always be possible, but the attempt should be made to boil away all but the essential. There will at first be considerable temptation to include too much in the outline for fear of passing over important points. Yet much of the specific knowledge the student must possess for the class meeting dealing with the assignment can safely be forgotten for the exam. There is a continual risk in studying law that the student will try to absorb too much material—that in working with a course he will try to learn everything, with the result that he will be unable to become the master of any of it. A completed outline for a course might be from fifty to one hundred pages long. Anything more could prove to be too unwieldy a mass of information when one studies for the exam.

Unless the professor has made a special point of emphasizing that a decision was handed down by a particular court and is unique for this reason, or that it is important because a certain judge espoused a novel theory or philosophy, or that the fact that an opinion was handed down in a given year was critical, the student need not record such factual information in his outline and need not remember it for an exam. Nor need he know or record the facts of the cases or the court's complete reasoning process. Furthermore, there are very few cases whose names or specific holdings must be remembered for an exam. It will be obvious from the professor's presentation or the casebook material which few cases are classic or major cases and therefore worth knowing for the semester. In these instances, the student will record the name of the case and its narrow holding in the outline. Several sentences discussing the reasoning of the court, or the reach of importance of the case, might also be included, but it would be a rare instance when the student had to consume more than a brief paragraph to capture in his outline the essence of a major case. In most other instances, merely the principles that the cases decided need be written out, if indeed they further the understanding of an area of law. From his class notes or casebook notes or underlinings, the student might include a particularly apt hypothetical or example that captures and elucidates the complexities of a subject, and of course the principles or blackletter law which the professor or casebook isolated should also be included. A student's outline will obviously be a very personal record of his work during a semester and of his understanding of a subject, but in general the outline should be neither so brief as to be enigmatic nor so lengthy as to merely repeat the information contained in the student's briefs and working notes. Each section of the outline should be clear enough to trigger the general ramifications of an area of law, but need not, and probably should not, set out every subtlety and complexity of each assignment.

In looking back on a block of material, determining what was most important in that material, and extracting those nuggets and setting them out in the outline occurs much of the intellectual process necessary to learn a body of law. At this point, with the greatest knowledge of, and clearest perspective on, an assignment, the student must win his professor's game of "hide the ball." Victory will be assured if the student has a sufficient grasp of the material in an assignment to set it out in a flexible outline form in his outline, with each new assignment classified under an appropriate heading and the material contained by that heading broken down into more specific classifications. For example, in a criminal law course an area of study will be homicide, which can be further broken into murder and manslaughter, with the murder section being divided into such classifications as malice aforethought, the felony murder rule, murder in the first degree, and murder in the second degree, and with the manslaughter section divided into such categories as voluntary manslaughter and involuntary manslaughter. The essential learning the student acquired about homicide can then be neatly filed away under its appropriate heading.

If it is not clear from the professor or the casebook exactly what type of classification an assignment's material should receive, some helpful ideas will be readily available by studying the casebook's table of contents or by turning to a treatise on the subject. Material should never just be dumped into an outline; to be a valuable study aid, it must be broken down into as specific classifications as is possible.

While he is making an outline and later as he studies it, the student will clearly see how what might have seemed like multiple, isolated, watertight compartments that made up a course actually mesh and work together quite logically.

The student ought to return to his outline regularly and reread it from page one. While there is no need to try to memorize it, the mere reading of the outline on a regular basis will develop in the student a deeper appreciation of the material and a keener familiarity with it. This will help put each succeeding case and class in context and will provide an opportunity for the student to reexamine his work to see if he has properly classified, or most appropriately classified, the earlier material. Revisions or refinements can continually be made when, for instance, the student sees that the material comprising several assignments could all be placed under a broader heading or that a section of material more clearly fell under a different classification.

Periodically, perhaps at two-week intervals, a running table of contents should be prepared for the outline. From this less immediate vantage point, the student will more readily perceive the interrelationships of the material. Including a simple table of contents with the outline will provide a key to the outline and the areas covered by the course and will be a convenient means of reviewing an entire course for the exam after the information in the outline has been learned.

In that the outline is the final distillation of what the student has judged to be of importance in a course, in that it will be the primary, even the exclusive, source of study for the exam in the course, the student will want to make it not only as substantively clear as is possible, but also as visually neat as possible. To this end, he should consider typing it, using good quality paper, and keeping it free of a jumble of arrows and stars and inserts. The outline, if well prepared, can also be the single most important source a student will study for his bar exam, and during his career can be a handy source for a quick overview of the law of a particular subject. The outline will in effect contain everything the student feels is worthy of taking away from a course to be made a part of his legal apparatus, and therefore should be prepared and treated as a permanent document.

Unless the student prepares his own outline, his exposure to the law of each course will be limited to his preparation for class, the class period, and his review at the end of the semester for the exams. With this limited exposure, it is usually not until the student begins to study for his exams that the scope of an area of law becomes obvious. As a result, the student is faced with a body of law that in a few days must be made comprehensible and then absorbed, a burdensome, and often futile, endeavor. Although the preparation of a valuable outline is an arduous process, all of the time and effort a student lavishes on it will pay a high return in mastery of a legal subject, and in making the exam for a course seem more like a natural and obvious conclusion of the semester than an insurmountable obstacle to fling oneself against blindly and in desperation.

EXAMS

"Ignorance of the law," it is said, "excuses no man." Certainly no law student. As the proof of the pudding is in the eating, so for all immediate practical purposes the proof of success in law school is in one's performance on the exams.

Just as admissions at most law schools are based on a formula combining LSAT scores and college grades to predict how an applicant will perform in law school, that is, how well he will do on his law school exams, so the career possibilities that will be open to a law school graduate will be determined to a large extent by the record he has achieved on his law school exams. While perhaps the only verifiable correlation between success on exams and success as an attorney is that the top law firm, clerkship, and teaching positions are filled with good test-takers, exams remain well entrenched as a way to quantify even some of the full range of qualities important in a good attorney.

Law school exam periods are always a time of anxiety, stress, and tension, and particularly so for the first-year student who, in addition to worrying that his semester grade for a course will be resting on a single three-hour examination, also suddenly finds himself face to face with a host of unknowns: whether he has been studying properly, whether he has studied enough, whether he has studied the right things, whether he has learned a course sufficiently for the purposes of an exam, what the exam will encompass. If the student has followed the types of procedures outlined in the preceding sections, he will probably feel as comfortable and confident about the substantive material of a course as possible. Without worrying about it constantly or making it an obsession, the student throughout the semester should also be attempting to find out all he can about the exam for a course so that it too will be a comfortably familiar challenge, rather than an obstacle of unknown proportions.

It is not too early to begin investigating the question of examinations within the first month of school, for the more a student discovers about what an exam will probably entail, the more closely he can gear his day-to-day work to that concrete goal.

Many law schools gather and bind together a copy of every exam given during each year. These volumes, often going back many years, will be shelved in the library or central administrative office. If after several weeks of class, when the student has gained a preliminary grasp of what a course is all about, he begins to read over the examinations his professor has given in the past, he will observe repeating patterns of emphasized material and typical sorts of questions, and so will begin to develop a feel for the type of exam the professor gives. For example, if a professor with predictable regularity thoroughly covers insanity and intoxication as defenses to criminal conduct, the student, while not being certain that such a question will appear on the forthcoming exam, may safely assume that the professor considers the area to be of importance and therefore will want to be prepared to deal with these areas on the exam. Similarly, if every semester for the past decade a professor sets forth his exam as a series of long, involved fact situations, or asks that the student assume the role of a lawyer for the defendant or plaintiff or the role of a judicial clerk and write a legal memorandum, the student will prepare in a different way than if the exams always consisted of pages of short-answer questions concerning the specific holdings of cases. And, although it is an ancient legal maxim that "the law is not concerned with trifles"—"de minimis non curat lex,"—the student should determine early in the game whether any of his law professors are concerned with trifles, or whether they are, for instance, more concerned with broad principles and theories.

If a law school does not make old exams available, or if a professor always excises his exams from the volumes, or if a professor is new to the school, the student will of course not be able to make as complete a survey of a professor's exam habits. But neither should he have to go into an exam cold. The student may want to speak to the professor about what type of exam could be expected and to ask if he would make any of his old exams available to the class. There are professors who wait until the final class period to talk about the exam and to announce that they are putting some sample exams on reserve in the library; such action comes much too late to help the student focus his studying toward the exams. The student must therefore often take the initiative to broach the subject of examinations, even at such an early stage of the semester that it might seem somewhat neurotic to be thinking about them. While the professor will probably not treat seriously questions like "Is *Brown* versus *Board of Education* going to be on the exam?" or "Do we have to know about guest statutes?" it would be reasonable to ask about the form of the exams and if the semester's material was going to be covered generally or if any particular areas were going to be emphasized or omitted. If a professor is unwilling to reveal anything about his exam, the student can still learn much about his style and focus by talking to upperclass students. If all else fails, exams for the same course given by other professors could be reviewed to gain a general idea of the types of questions that might be involved.

Whether there will be a generous reading period between the end of classes and the beginning of exams, and whether the exams will be well-spaced with free days between each will depend on the policies of the individual law school and the fates which decide the student's individual exam schedule. Exam schedules are not customarily announced too far in advance of the examinations, so the student should be prepared for the worst: an inadequate reading period, if any at all, and all exams bunched together.

There are students who by nature tend toward delay and procrastination and who will put off the drudgery of mastering each course until right before the examinations. Whether or not the effect of a splurge of all-nighters spent cramming a semester of law into reeling brains is evident in their blue books, it is at least evident in themselves as they walk through the law school as tight as finely-drawn violin strings or as dazed as victims of shock. However successful the student has been with such last-minute efforts in college, he should hold them in abeyance at least during the first year in law school, for a midnight attempt to absorb for the first time a massive and hazy body of law is an experience better avoided.

On the other hand, if the student has been preparing outlines for each course, returning to them weekly to revise, review, and update, the hardest part of his work will have ended with the final class period. He will already have a working familiarity with the organization and the substance of the material, and through his weekly readings will discover that—without any conscious effort to memorize the material—by a process of osmosis this knowledge has already become safely implanted in a new set of brain grooves and conceptual receptacles. Rather than having to learn the material afresh at the end of the semester, the student has the opportunity to polish his knowledge to the finished degree necessary to write superior exams.

Approximately five or six weeks before the examination period, the student can begin to prepare in earnest. Tackling one course each week, he could divide the number of pages in his outline by the number of days of the week he will study the subject, and then carefully study and review that number of pages of his outline each day. By dividing an outline into this type of bite-size portion, the student can sharply focus his attention on the material without adding an impossible burden to his continuing day-to-day class work.

If the outline has been carefully prepared, there will be few instances, if any, when the student will have to return to his notes, briefs, or casebooks for clarification. All of these sources are now best put aside. Concentration should now be exclusively on the outline. It should be learned so thoroughly that it is almost memorized, not in the sense that the student sets out to commit it to memory, but in the sense that the information is so familiar and so well understood that the student can turn to the table of contents he has made for his outline and from those key words and phrases flesh out all the major ideas and concepts, cases and principles contained in the outline under those categories. This daily review should continue up to the day of the examination, with the entire outline reviewed the day before the exam.

It should now be clear why the outline must be a compact document capable of easy assimilation, and clear also how a student can readily "learn" a self-prepared outline while really only memorizing a commercially-prepared outline or an outline prepared by another member of a study group.

This method of review should be followed for each course, even in those rare instances when a professor announces that his exam will be open-book or open-notes. It can be stated with absolute certainty that unless a student is as familiar with the material of a course as he would be for a regular exam, the fact that an exam is open-book will be of no help to him and may even be harmful if it engenders a sense of complacency which cuts down his preparation and review. There will simply be no time during the exam to look up information that the student has not already classified and absorbed.

The typical law school exam consists of several intricate fact situations followed by a general type of question such as "Discuss and evaluate the rights, liabilities, and remedies of the parties," or "Discuss what crimes may be charged, against whom and defenses thereto," or "What steps would you take in the trial court on behalf of the defendant at this stage? What supporting arguments would you make?" In this type of exam, as in most other types of law school exams, the professor is looking less for "the solution" to the problem, in the sense of what a court might decide, than he is looking for the student's ability to spot the issues and ambiguities of the problem and to suggest approaches to resolve them.

The professor is not interested in reading an involved introduction to the student's answer, nor will he be interested, unless specifically requested, in reading a general essay on a particular aspect of the law with only a vague connection with the problem on the exam. Writes Professor Walter B. Raushenbush of the University of Wisconsin Law School:

A few years ago, in a course in Real Estate Transactions, the first question in the exam I drafted stated that "A" and "B" entered into a "valid written contract" for the sale of Blackacre by "A" to "B." The question went on to give the essentials of the contract, to describe the difficulties between the parties, and to ask for a legal resolution of the difficulties. Believe it or not, nearly half the students began by writing me a considerable essay on the requirements of the Statute of Frauds, pointing out that the contract between "A" and "B" complied with the Statute.

Of course it did; I told them in the question that it was a valid written contract. But you see, we had studied the Statute of Frauds early in the course. Apparently their intensive review had got them at least that far. Naturally too, something that came early in the course would be in the first question! They got no credit for their essays on the Statute of Frauds, but the effort had a fine cathartic effect on them: In a later question involving a very real Statute of Frauds problem, most of them missed it.[32]

The aim of the law student is therefore not to discuss the law in abstract terms or to attempt to find the one and only answer to a hypothetical, but to be able to recognize and discuss all the issues and problems lurking within or behind the facts. It is this ability which most professors regard as the hallmark of the mastery of a course.

Thus, to take an absurd example to make the point, as a torts student reads through a hypothetical patterned after the nursery tale of "Goldilocks and the Three Bears," he would mentally check off the various issues called forth by the facts. Has Goldilocks trespassed as to the bears' property and house? Is there a conversion question with her eating their porridge? Did she exercise due care in sitting in the baby bear's chair? Does Goldilocks have any possible actions against the bears? Are they liable for assault by surrounding her as she slept? Would they be liable for intentional infliction of mental distress? Are bears in general, and the baby bear in particular, to be held to human standards of care? What type of privilege did the bears have to protect their property? Could the bears have set traps on their land to discourage trespassing? What types of incentives do the courts want to foster: to feel secure in one's home? to protect trespassers from harm?

Having carefully read over the problem marking those phrases or facts that catalyze the issues and problems within the hypothetical, and having taken a few minutes to outline briefly the answer that seems to be called for, the student should launch right into the answer, perhaps starting by writing, "The first issue is whether . . ." By spotting the issues the professor meant to raise and by analyzing the problems to which they give rise, the student will be on the right track in dealing with the question. The student should beware of answering one of the issues in such a manner that the entire fact situation is immediately resolved, thus curtailing his analysis. If one issue seems critical to the case but its outcome is debatable, the student should point out that the case could be resolved in a certain fashion, but if it was not, then the following additional issues would have to be considered. In other words, the student should exercise great care to deal with all the issues fairly raised by the facts without taking broad liberties with the given facts to invent and resolve issues not squarely contained in the problem. A one-sided approach to an issue should be avoided; rather, persuasive reasons supporting both sides shold be discussed. Above all, the issues raised and the law applied should always be tightly bound to the particular facts of the case.

Each answer should show an understanding of the facts, the issues involved, and the applicable principles of law. Each answer should demonstrate not merely the student's memory, but the process of reasoning by which he worked with the facts, issues, and law to arrive at a conclusion. Each answer should be clear, concise, grammatical, and presented in a well-organized and logical style.

Latent or patent, law schools are institutions which are fairly seething with competition. This competition can manifest itself in most destructive forms at exam time. The tension students feel during these periods is easily communicable and there are some who, for whatever reasons, will try to intensify this already oppressive atmosphere. For example, one professor, who as a law student always typed his exams, admitted that as soon as an exam was handed out he would put a sheet of paper into his typewriter and begin pounding away nonsense sentences. Naturally, all the other students in the room were convinced that he had instantly perceived the nature of the first question, developed an answer, and was well on his way to completion, and so worried about their own inability to tackle the exam as quickly.

More commonly, a half hour or so before an exam begins the air will be buzzing with frantic questions about the facts of a case or the five elements that constitute adverse possession. There are those who specialize in spending these last minutes before an exam asking involved questions of those around them, slyly implying that if a person can't immediately dredge up the answer, he is going to find the approaching exam rough going. If a student has a tendency to be disturbed or jogged by such tactics, he might want to be studiously reading something or safely sequestered in an out-of-the-way spot until the last possible moment. One should at least be aware that such obnoxious, often dangerously subtle, stratagems can come into play during the final days or hours before an exam.

One persistent criticism of the law school examination process is that all the student learns about his performance on an exam is a single letter or number grade. It is unusual for a professor to hand back the graded exams or to meet with the class to discuss the types of answers he was seeking. It is therefore possible for the student to go through three years of law school writing the same type of examinations and receiving the same type of grades.

If the student truly does not understand why he received a particular grade, or is uncertain as to how he could have written a better exam, he should see his professor as soon after the grades are posted as possible. Some professors might be willing to go over his exam with him and discuss ways in which it could have been improved, but at a minimum the student should be allowed to read a blue book that the professor considered well done. After a careful reading, the student might then have some specific questions which the professor could more easily answer than the general lament, "Where did I go wrong?"

First-semester exams can have a definite effect on the personality of one's colleagues. Often, without even knowing the grades a person received, it will be obvious from his new sense

of confidence and ease that he did well and that his faith in his
own intellect, bruised and buffeted during the initial months
of law school, has been reaffirmed. Those who did not do as
well as they had hoped should take care not to be caught in a
web of despair and self-doubt. It is certainly true that more
people leave law school because of self-generated tension than
because of unacceptable grades. If a person has put in a consci-
entious semester's work, he will at least have a better understanding of what law school requires and of what he can do to
improve his performance.

The student should also realize that the relationship between the grade he received and his mastery of a course might
be a rather tenuous one. One of the inequities of first-year law
school is that the students are usually assigned their course
and professors. When there are several sections of a required
first-year course taught by different professors, there might
well be vast differences in what the sections learn and what
kinds of grades the sections receive on the examination. Thus,
an examination graded "C" by a professor who taught one
first-year contracts section might have been awarded a "B" or
an "A" by a professor who taught another section of contracts
and who did not believe all first-year exams should be graded
low to terrorize students into working even harder. Similarly,
one contracts section might have received a thorough ground-
ing in standard contracts law while another section, placed by
fate in a class taught by a professor who wished to experiment
with a new way of teaching contracts, might end the semester
in a state of confusion if the professor's experiment failed.
There is little that may be done about such inequities except
to grin and bear it, perhaps with the inner satisfaction of knowing that while justice might be slow, it is sure. One year the
faculty of a southern law school was depleted by several leaves
of absence with the result that the important course of commercial transactions was offered by only one professor. At the
end of the semester when grades were posted, the captive

students of this class were shocked to discover that almost all had received "C's" on the examination. The professor's field of expertise was quickly labeled "The Law of the C" and for several years thereafter this reputation haunted him. He found that instead of teaching classes of a hundred or more students as he was accustomed, his elective classes were selected by only a meager handful of students who hadn't received the word. Through such a judicious selection of courses and professors, upperclass students can see that the inequities of the first year are balanced out.

While the benefits of a top first-semester or first-year performance are substantial, most employers are cognizant of the special problems inherent in the first year and are inclined to be tolerant of a less than superior first-year record if the student shows improvement during the following semesters. And if, after several semesters, the student discovers that despite his best efforts he is in a law school where it is impossible for him to be at the top of the class, he might call to mind the old law school maxim that those who receive the "A's" become law professors, those who receive "B's" will become judges, and those who receive anything else will be the ones who make all the money.

Some credence might indeed be given to this theory by the first-year law school experience of the King of Torts, Melvin Belli. "At first I didn't know how to write an exam and drew an early C in Torts and another C in Contracts."[33] Belli of course went on to become one of the most celebrated, and highest paid, lawyers of this century. But perhaps the important lesson to be drawn from Belli's experience is that how to take an exam, and, more generally, how to study law, involve skills and talents which are native to very few, and which must be consciously cultivated and developed by most students. "By the end of the third year," Belli reports, "I was number thirteen in my class, with straight A's in Criminal Law, Property, and the toughest courses."[34] Belli had not suddenly acquired a

legal mind. He had learned between his first and final years at
law school how to apply his native intelligence to the study of
law. He had learned how to study law.

PRACTICING LAW

It has been said that the only job for which a student is qualified after three years of law school is that of a justice of the
Supreme Court of the United States.

Having spent three years briefing, analyzing, and discussing
appellate court opinions, the student has a solid background in
the end-product of the judicial process. But, as law school edu-
cators are fond of remarking, he will not have been taught how
to pack his briefcase or how to find the courthouse, a benign
way of recognizing the troublesome fact that the student's experience in dealing with clients, in legal research and writing, in
trial and appellate advocacy, in short, in all the practical skills it
takes to be a lawyer if one happened not to be offered a seat on
the Supreme Court upon graduation, is *de minimis*. As the lord
chief justice of England recently commented, too often the fledg-
ling lawyer "finds himself standing alone in the middle of a
courtroom like a matador facing his first bull, and probably
profoundly wishing that he had taken his father's advice to become an automobile salesman instead."[35]

Upon completion of law school, the graduate will begin
practicing law, in every sense of the word practicing. The bar
has been spoken of as "the only profession where a person is
qualified to carry on his business without ever having seen it
conducted or knowing from the practical point of view how it
is done. It may be that medical students are allowed to do too
many things to the public before they are qualified, but at
least there is a good deal of control over them and they are not
licensed to kill. As soon as you are qualified [as a lawyer] you

are, and if you win any cases in your first year it will be Providence and not you who secures the verdict for your client."[36]

Surely any lawyer could illustrate the point with examples from his own early practice. Clark Clifford, former Secretary of Defense, presidential advisor, Washington lawyer, recalled his first case:

> [It] involved a man named John Piper, who was charged with stealing an automobile. I spent three days trying his case. And oh, but did I prepare! I read the life of Clarence Darrow and other famous criminal lawyers, and I wrote out a ringer of a jury speech.
>
> The jury went out and came back in fifteen minutes and gave John Piper twenty years. I was crushed. I thought my career was at an end. The judge saw I was hurt, and he called me up and said he was going to appoint me to another case right away. I started to protest, because I didn't want any more, but he stopped me. "Clark," he said, "it's like getting thrown from a horse or going down in a plane. You've got to get right back up or you'll be gunshy and never do it again." So I took another case, and wow-ee! Boy! They sent him up again!
>
> All this time I kept trying to forget poor John Piper. This poor fellow—he wasn't much older than I was, and there he sat, in the state penitentiary. I did my best to forget it, but each Christmas, just about the time I thought I'd forgotten about him, here would come a Christmas card from poor old John Piper in the state pen.
>
> I kept on trying cases, and getting licked, until my twelfth or fourteenth came along, and I got a verdict—'I sprung one,' was the expression—and man, did I feel good. It was like being thrown into the creek by your dad to learn to swim; you consume an awful lot of water, but you learn how to swim.
>
> An interne has to work on people to become a doctor, and he sends some to the graveyard. Well, I sent mine to the state penitentiary.[37]

As Clark Clifford and every young lawyer learns, the only way an attorney can develop his professional skills is through the very practice of law. The amount of ground to be covered in a three-year legal education is already so extensive that there is no time to equip the student with the techniques of trying a case, of handling an appeal, or of any of the multitude of practical skills necessary to practice law, even if such skills could be transmitted through the regular educational process. The one important exception is the ability to do sophisticated legal research and writing. It is this skill that the student must perfect while still in law school.

Legal research is the very foundation of the practice of law, for whether the lawyer be advising a client or handling a suit through the courts, he must know as precisely as possible what the law is. Even more difficult, the lawyer, after discovering what the law is, must then be able to forecast the trends of the law, for very often what a client really wants to know is not what the law is today, but what it will be at the time the problem under discussion is likely to come up for adjudication in the courts. This is what Mr. Justice Holmes had in mind when he said, "Prophecies of what the courts will do in fact, and nothing more pretentious, are what I mean by the law." Legal research is the one area in which the young lawyer can match even an experienced opponent, and quite often the young lawyer can bring more concentration and prolonged labor to the heavy chore of research than can his more experienced adversary; once the basic skills have been acquired, the result will depend solely on the degree of care, precision, and tenacity with which an attorney attacks a problem. On a solid facility for legal research, a law school graduate can readily construct and develop the other attributes and skills of a qualified attorney.

Most law schools offer a superficial law library orientation program in conjunction with a first-year legal writing course. The student should be warned that any lecture on the use of a law library, or any reading about the techniques of legal research, will probably at first be devoid of much meaning, if even intelligible. Although Lord Edward Coke proclaimed that "the law is the perfection of reason," any initial feelings the first-year student might have been harboring about the truth of Dickens' classic pronouncement in *Oliver Twist* that "the law is a ass—a idiot," any feelings that might have been developing within him that the law is an impenetrable jungle, a hostile wilderness, are likely to be solidified and crystallized during his first encounters with a law library and legal research.

In 1955, it was estimated that the number of reported American decisions exceeded 2,100,000 and was increasing at the rate of 22,000 published decisions each year. In comparison, there were 5,000 opinions available to the legal profession of Coke's and Bacon's seventeenth century and only 10,000 English decisions 150 years later in the days of Mansfield and Blackstone. In comparison, in 1953 the Congress and forty-eight state legislatures enacted 29,938 statutes to add to the 931 volumes of existing statutes. Furthermore, during the same period federal administrative regulations were contained in over 41 volumes, and the annual reported decisions of only four of the multitude of federal administrative agencies exceeded in volume the reports of all the federal courts of appeal and district courts. To this plethora of official legal publications must be added the legal digests, encyclopedias, loose-leaf services, law reviews, and casebooks which perpetually pour off the presses. It hardly needs to be added that in the years since the mid-1950s, the sheer bulk of written law has increased explosively. For example, the number of criminal cases in federal courts rose 25 percent between 1964 and 1974 and during the same period civil case filings jumped by 55 percent. The business in state courts has grown apace, if not even more swiftly.[38] Today, legislative bodies of every size across the United States spew forth new laws at the rate of about 100,000 per year, and federal agencies are generating an additional 35,000 or more new regulations a year.[39]

This mushrooming mass of law has led to repeated calls throughout this century for codification, but to date the work of the American Law Institute and the National Conference of Commissioners on Uniform State Laws to restate, clarify, and simplify the law has covered only a small portion of the corpus of American law. The use of computers to facilitate legal research looms as a potential solution to prevent the law from collapsing under its own weight, but the initial expenses involved in programming have inhibited their widespread use in the legal profession. While still in its infancy, computer-assisted legal research in which a lawyer can conduct a continuing dialogue with the computer by means of a communications terminal in his office will, with improved flexibility, ease of use, reliability, and speed, undoubtedly be the wave of the future. But even in that brave new world, the computer will be only as good as the lawyer who operates it and the legal research skills the lawyer possesses.

A thorough facility with the techniques of legal research, coupled with the physical strength and mental resolution to scale the mountain ranges of reported judicial decisions and statutes, therefore still remains the most essential tool of a lawyer's professional equipment.

Not only is the sheer volume of the law overwhelming, but also the methods that have been developed to extract the law from the endless aisles of judicial records might, at first encounter, seem hostile and impenetrable. Far from unlocking the secrets of the law, these sources referred to as entry points into the law—a jumble of digests, encyclopedias, citators, reporters, indexes, quick indexes, annotations, codes, treatises, pocket parts, supplements, key numbers, loose-leaf services, reviews, slip decisions, restatements, and tables—might seem to exist solely as a labyrinth to impede one's search for appropriate precedent.

Regardless of initial appearances, the student, after he has gained some practical experience with the use of a law library, will perceive the inherent logic and utility of the existing system of legal research. He will undoubtedly conclude that the real wonder of the law is that a system of entry was able to be developed that operates so efficiently and expeditiously, and that the seemingly impassable mountains of recorded law have been so well surveyed and their topography so carefully charted.

For simplicity, the legal literature with which lawyers are most concerned in their work may be classified into two categories: primary and secondary sources. Primary source materials include court opinions, congressional acts and legislative statutes, executive orders, regulations of administrative agencies, and rules of court. These materials are of either binding legal effect or persuasive force and therefore are those on which the lawyer places primary reliance in preparing a legal memorandum or brief. Secondary source materials include such texts as legal encyclopedias, treatises, and law reviews. These sources may serve as valuable aids in explaining the law or in providing a basic understanding of, or creative insight into, a particular segment of the law, and may also serve as case finders, that is, as points of entry into primary source materials. Also, a passage from a secondary source may serve as an excellent way to introduce a discussion of the more specific primary authorities, or as a means of substantiating axiomatic statements of broad legal principles.

Federal and state appellate court opinions and federal and state statutes are the most important primary sources of legal authority to which the lawyer must daily turn. Judicial opinions are gathered together in chronological volumes. The *United States Reporter* is the official edition of the United States Supreme Court decisions, while the *Supreme Court Reporter* and the *Lawyers' Edition of the United States Supreme Court Reporter* are privately published editions of the Supreme Court's decisions which also include additional special research aids and supplementary materials. The *Federal*

Reporter contains all the decisions of the various United States Courts of Appeal, and the *Federal Supplement* publishes selected United States District Court decisions. The reports of the state courts are published in official reporters issued by each of the states, and also in an unofficial *National Reporter System* which divides the United States into seven regions and publishes together the state reports comprising each particular region.

To discover on-point cases, that is, cases that are factually or legally similar to the problem the lawyer is attempting to solve, from over three million chronologically reported cases, the researcher must turn first to case digests. Multivolume case digests divide the body of the law into several hundred topical categories which are arranged alphabetically, and which in turn are divided into thousands of subclassifications. Very brief abstracts of every principle of law contained in every reported case are grouped together under the appropriate subject classification. Through a detailed index of legally significant descriptive catch words, the researcher can locate the appropriate legal classification, which is assigned a key number, and then focus on the most relevant abstracts listed under this classification.

Indexes are the lawyer's initial point of entry into these case digests, as well as into all other legal sources, and the use the lawyer makes of them will determine the quality of his research. One method of using such indexes is to consider the problem or issue that is pending and then, before opening the index, to make a list of all the words, and their synonyms, which the problem or issue suggests—that is, the various things, acts, persons or places without which there could have been no controversy. Then, the lawyer may turn to the index and note whatever references appear for each word or phrase he has listed. Otherwise, if the researcher were to open the index first to the most obvious word and find no such listing, he would be tempted to conclude that there was no material on his topic of concern. For example, for purposes of illustration the West Publishing Company, which publishes the digests, presents the hypothetical situation of a referee at a professional wrestling match who is thrown from the ring in such a way that he strikes and injures a front row spectator. In analyzing the problem, the researcher, in turning to the descriptive word index of the case digest, might consider the parties involved and look under "spectator," "patron," "arena owner," "wrestler," "referee" or "promoter;" might consider the places and things involved and look under "wrestling match," "amusement place," "theater," or "show;" might consider the basis of action or issue and look under "negligence," "personal injury to spectator," or "liability;" might consider the defense and look under "assumption of risk;" or might consider the relief sought and look under "damages." Thus, even by approaching a problem from a number of different angles, the researcher should be led to the same result.

There are a number of different case digests covering different jurisdictions. For example, the *American Digest System* covers all decisions in all the regional reporter systems, the *United States Supreme Court Digest* covers all Supreme Court cases, and most of the states have individual state digests. The same system of topic classifications and subclassifications are used in all the digests, so that the researcher can move easily among them. Thus, if the courts in a particular jurisdiction have had little or nothing to say on a particular subject, or if the question is one of first impression, or if the lawyer is tidying up a confused field of law, the gaps can readily be filled in, or buttresses formed, with persuasive authority from other jurisdictions. Once the researcher has located the appropriate topic and its assigned key number, he has ready access to all American cases that have litigated the issue by turning to the same key number in every other case digest.

With approximately 30,000 new judicial decisions rendered each year and at least 10,000 new statutes annually enacted,[40] it is obvious that the law is in a constant state of flux and change. It would seem to be a perverse truism of legal research that the one opinion or statute which serves as the critical linchpin of the lawyer's argument, will, unless carefully checked, prove to have been just overturned, reversed, modified, or repealed, thus rendering his entire memorandum or brief worthless.

Fortunately, an ingenious method of avoiding such problems has been developed through the use of *Shepard's Citations*, indexes which list the citation to every published opinion folowed by the citation of every later published decision citing that opinion. These indexes are kept current with pamphlet supplements, and through them the lawyer may quickly verify the current status of a case or a statute to determine whether it is still effective law or whether its authority has been diminished or destroyed. It is imperative that every legal citation in a legal document prepared by the researcher be Shepardized to ascertain its current status and relevance.

In addition, Shepardizing a case or statute enables the researcher to trace the judicial treatment and history of cases and the judicial construction and legislative history of the statutes he is using, and thus discloses many later, additional cases that might otherwise never be discovered. Through the use of *Shepard's Citations*, the researcher may discover every opinion that has cited a given case or statute, thus giving him immediate access to how a law or legal principle has been analyzed and interpreted.

Statutes are of mandatory authority in the jurisdiction where enacted. Although statutes, like judicial opinions, are published chronologically in separate volumes, there are also unofficial compilations by topic, such as in the *United States Code Annotated*. Through detailed indexes the researcher is led to the particular sections dealing with his area of concern. Such compilations are often annotated with court decisions construing, interpreting, and applying the various statutory sections, with statements of the legislative history of the laws, and with references to other treatise sections concerned with the statute and how it has been construed. As with court opinions, all statutes relied upon or cited in a legal document should be Shepardized to verify their current status and also to locate cases which have dealt with them.

With the growth of administrative agencies since the Second World War, the orders, regulations and decisions of federal and state agencies have played an increasingly important role in a lawyer's work. If a legal problem could conceivably fall within the ambit of an agency's jurisdiction, it would be necessary to survey the relevant decisions and rulings of that agency, be it the Internal Revenue Service or a state public utilities commission.

There are two sets of secondary source books which are the lawyer's equivalent of encyclopedias: *American Jurisprudence* and *Corpus Juris Secundum*. Just as the *Encyclopaedia Britannica* and the *World Book Encyclopedia* are comprised of a multitude of articles on the various branches of knowledge arranged in alphabetical order, so *Am. Jur.* and *C.J.S.* are multivolume sets, differing essentially only in style, covering all aspects of the law. These legal encyclopedias can serve a useful function in providing a general overview of a field of law and in leading the researcher to other secondary authorities or to on-point case citations which open avenues of more thorough research. Rapid entry may be gained to both encyclopedias through detailed indexes in which the researcher can often pinpoint the precise issue with which he is concerned. Both sets contain annual pocket supplements which update the treatment of various topics.

Another legal encyclopedia is *Words and Phrases*, an encyclopedia of definitions of legally significant words including citations to, and abstracts of, cases that have interpreted or construed the words and phrases.

The *American Law Reports (A.L.R.)* contains selected, significant judicial opinions followed by thorough, often exhaus-

tive, annotations or discussions of the law of the case. For
example, there is a 53-page annotation at 83 *A.L.R. 3d* 458
concerning "Dissolution of Corporation on Grounds of Intra-
corporate Deadlock or Dissension," and a 113-page annotation
at 55 *A.L.R. 2d* 6 entitled "Implied or Apparent Authority of
an Agent to Purchase or Order Goods or Merchandise." When
the lawyer discovers an on-point annotation through the indexes to *A.L.R.*, *A.L.R. 2d*, *A.L.R. 3d* or *A.L.R. Federal*, he
will have access to a detailed analysis of the current law in all
states on the particular problem, the general principles of law
deduced from the case and their exceptions, limitations, quali-
fications, distinctions and applications, and citations to on-
point cases from all states. It might be noted that there are few
United States Supreme Court cases annotated in *A.L.R.* since
they are annotated in the *Lawyers' Edition of the United
States Supreme Court Reporter*.

Treatises, such as Corbin on *Contracts*, Prosser on *Torts*,
Davis on *Administrative Law*, and Wigmore on *Evidence*, are
narrowly focused on particular areas of the law, but like legal
encyclopedias present a detailed review of that particular area.
There are numerous treatises on a multitude of substantive
and procedural legal topics; they may be located through a law
library's card catalogue system or by browsing in the treatise
alcove. Although their quality varies, courts often place considerable reliance on the discussion of peculiar developments
of the law presented in leading treatises by eminent scholars,
and all can prove helpful in making comprehensible an unfamiliar legal topic. Similarly, a relevant law review article,
which may be located through the *Index to Legal Periodicals*,
may prove to be useful in gaining deeper insight into a legal
problem.

Depending upon the depth to which a lawyer wishes to
pursue a problem or the novelty of the problem he is research-
ing, there is a host of other more specialized primary and
secondary sources he may wish to consult, in addition to a

world of nonlegal scholarship if the lawyer wishes to take a more eclectic approach to a legal problem and examine, for example, the social and economic consequences of laws and legal policies. In general, the degree to which a lawyer chooses to research a problem will depend on how much time he can bring to his work and how quickly he becomes convinced of the solidity of his grasp of the relevant law.

The key to unlocking the secrets of a law library and the techniques of legal research is to go into the law library and start "bouncing off the walls"—to take free moments to wander up and down the aisles, to go to the case digests, skim through them, and see how they operate, to use them to look up a case that is to be read for the next day, to try to locate on-point opinions from the jurisdiction in which the student expects to practice, to determine if a decision has been reversed or modified and how frequently it has been cited, to look up a statute on a subject of interest to the student, to thumb through the principal primary and secondary sources until it becomes obvious how they are set up and organized—in other words, to become as familiar as possible with the diverse and extensive range of resources a law library contains.

Similarly, to pick up the special methods and styles of legal writing and to see how legal research is set forth in writing, the first-year student will want to become a regular reader of law review articles and notes. A good starting point might be either the law review of his law school or a law review which covers the law of the state in which he expects to practice.

Thoroughness, speed, and above all, accuracy are the qualities the researcher must bring to his work. The need for meticulous accuracy and perfection in legal research cannot be overstressed. Whether a research problem involves an analysis of a single case, the application of a settled legal doctrine to a new set of facts, or the development of a creative or novel legal solution to a unique factual pattern, the opportunities for the researcher to go astray are legion. Every lawyer must have at least one personal story of a critical case overlooked, an opinion misconstrued, a statute misread, or a document not carefully proofread, with disastrous results. Charles Evans Hughes, while clerking in 1883 in the New York City firm of Chamberlain, Carter & Hornblower, had just such an experience which years later stood out vividly in his memory even after his successful careers as a prominent lawyer, Governor of New York, Supreme Court Justice, Secretary of State, a member of the World Court, and Chief Justice of the United States.

Mr. Hornblower [a senior partner of the firm] was in the midst of a vexatious litigation over the assets of an insolvent firm and he was opposed by one E. Payson Wilder, a terror of the New York bar. Hornblower and Wilder were up and down in the courts, fighting savagely with motions, appeals, etc. Wilder never failed to begin his argument by saying—"My friend, Mr. Blowhorner, I beg pardon, Mr. Hornblower," which would make the latter livid with rage. On a certain Friday, Mr. Hornblower, leaving for his place in the country, left with Bowers [the managing clerk] the proof of a brief which was to be printed and in readiness on Monday morning. Mr. Hornblower had a liking for emphatic printing and used italics, capitals and boldface freely. In this brief, he reached the summit of his argument in an outstanding line, "And the firm paid *seven thousand dollars* in CASH." On Monday morning, the brief neatly printed was on his desk, but soon we heard his quick step down the hall and he appeared at the clerk's door so full of wrath that he could hardly speak. He pointed to the climax in his brief, which to our amazement and horror read, "And the firm paid *seven thousand dollars* in COAL." Bowers and I did not know which of us was responsible for this egregious error, whether it was due to a misreading of Mr. Hornblower's script or to a failure to catch the mistake in print, and we both took Hornblower's unsparing denunciation with abject humility and contrition. Thenceforth, I was the most careful of proofreaders, quite sure that the mistake most likely to be overlooked would be on the title page or in some conspicuous place where it would stand out like a monument.[41]

As Hughes learned, eternal vigilance is the price of accuracy. The greatest care must be exercised during every stage of legal research.

In that legal writing deals with the practical skills that will have immediate application in any type of law-related work, prospective employers will in many instances be more interested in what grade the student received in his legal writing course than in any other course. The student will therefore want to devote as much time to preparing the assigned memoranda and briefs or to preparing for oral argument as will be necessary to perform to the best of his abilities. Often an employer will ask for a sample of the student's legal writing. A well-prepared memo or brief can be a strong selling point. The student will of course wish to keep a copy of all of his legal writings for these purposes, duplicating the original before it is turned in and marked up by his professor. Similarly, when the student decides whether to join any extracurricular law school activities, it should be kept in mind that those activities which stress legal research, legal writing, and advocacy skills—such as work on a law review or legal journal (the scholarly legal periodicals of the legal profession prepared at every law school by the top students of the upper classes), or participation in a moot court competition (which involves preparation of briefs and participation in an oral argument on a fictitious legal issue, usually with one or more professors acting as the judge)—will be viewed most favorably by prospective employers as further evidence of the student's working knowledge, as opposed to purely academic knowledge, of the law. Again, a copy of any legal writing the student has done should be kept and submitted with the student's résumé as a sample of his best work.

There is little disagreement that whatever time the student can devote to becoming acquainted with the tools of legal research will be profitably spent, for proficiency in the law invariably depends on access to its resources and an ability to mine from those resources the pure gold of legal principles.

CONCLUSION

In their less guarded moments, law professors have been known to admit that out of each entering class, there will be only several students who really enjoy their law school experience. For the rest, a legal education is somewhat like military service: something that at best is endured.

Unfortunately, this estimate would indeed seem to be a close approximation of the truth. Lord Chancellor Eldon's proverbial advice to law students that the only way to become barristers was to "make up their minds to live like hermits and work like horses"[42] captures something of the total commitment the student must make to his work. Nevertheless, although the pace of law school is fast and the amount of ground to be covered enormous, although the student will probably work harder in law school than he ever has before, and although the work can become repetitious and tedious on some occasions during the three years, there is nothing inherent in a legal education that should prevent it from being a challenging, stimulating, and enjoyable experience.

"The law school," it has been said by the eminent legal scholar Bernard Schwartz, "remains the only place where most lawyers have an opportunity to think about the law in anything like the grand manner."[43] By understanding the requirements and demands of a legal education, and so avoiding much of the initial confusion and uncertainty associated with beginning law school, the student can immediately apply his full talents to his work and achieve a successful law school record. He will also have the opportunity to appreciate more keenly and enjoy more completely the challenge and excitement that should be a part of a successful legal education.

The Art of Advocacy

There are two distinct parts to the lawyer's work in court. The first is the presentation of evidence on direct, cross- and redirect examination, a great art in itself; but the evidence alone would often fail to attain full significance without the other phase of the advocate's work—skill in forensic persuasion, which enables him to make the most of the evidence. These matters are the heart of the lawyer's work. His client's life or liberty or his property interests depend on his ability to do both tasks well. Nor is this all; on his skill in the presentation of his case in court the course of the development of the law may turn, for the courts must necessarily rely largely on the research of counsel in reaching their decisions. Yet oddly enough, the arts of forensic persuasion are not taught in any of our law schools. So hard pressed for time are we in imparting knowledge of the law and in teaching skill in legal reasoning that the acquisition of the great arts of the advocate is left to chance as if there were neither art nor science in the matter.

There are some very definite laws, prescribed by neither the courts nor the legislature, that govern the effective presentation of every case in court quite as much as if they were

written in the statute book or embodied in the rules of court.
These laws may seem to vary as one moves from the opening
of a case to the summing-up after all the evidence is in. They
may seem to differ when there is a jury present from what
they are when the judge sits alone as both the trier of the facts
and the arbiter of the law. There may seem to be little in
common between an opening and summation and the remarks
that counsel addresses to the court on objections to the recep-
tion of his adversary's evidence, or on a motion for a nonsuit at
the end of a plaintiff's case, or for a directed verdict at the
close of the entire case. There may also seem to be little
resemblance between any of these steps in a trial and a motion
for a new trial after a jury has come in with an adverse verdict.
Even more set apart may seem to be the argument of an
appeal from the judgment below to a reviewing court, which is
everywhere deemed to be the crown of the advocate's work.
Yet in all these various types of forensic persuasion there is an
essential unity; the outward differences merely reflect either
the differences in the tribunal addressed or the purpose for
which it is addressed. This essential unity springs from the
nature of the human mind. In each step we are dealing with
the impact of one mind on another in an effort to resolve a
controversy between human beings according to certain very
definite rules of fair play that have for their grand objective the
substitution of reason for force. When the process works, we
achieve justice; when it fails, we must write it down as a
failure of your profession and mine.

Most of these successive steps in the forensic presentation
of a case emphasize the constructive phase of the advocate's
activities; he is endeavoring to synthesize the facts and the
applicable law from his client's point of view and to make the
most of them. It is work that often reveals the lawyer at his
best. The pleadings, his trial brief, even his appellate brief
may seem cold and detached, as by their inexorable logic he
seeks to demonstrate to the judicial mind the soundness of

his client's position. But from the very fact that lawyers and judges and jurors are men, every word that the advocate utters in the courtroom, whether in opening to the jury or in arguing to the court of last resort, will inevitably be permeated, for better or worse, by the influence of his personality, however much the wise advocate may seek to subordinate it to the facts and the law of his case. Every word that the lawyer addresses to the court or the jury is intended not merely to convince, but to persuade—to move the court or the jury to take a desired action, action I may add that is always at the expense of the adverse party. The competitive spirit prevailing in the trial court or in the appellate tribunal, although always restrained within the limits of forensic decorum, cannot fail to quicken the pulse of the true advocate and to give him an exhilaration and glow—win, lose, or draw—that cannot be equalled by any other intellectual activity of our profession.

THE SIX FACTORS IN THE WORK OF THE ADVOCATE

Before proceeding to discuss in some detail the various types of forensic persuasion to which I have alluded, it will be helpful to enumerate and then to comment briefly on the six factors that are involved in the work of the advocate.

1. The capacity for grasping all the facts of a case in all of their interrelations and implications quickly and comprehensively.
2. A thorough understanding of the fundamental principles and rules of law and the ability to apply them to the facts of a case.
3. Knowledge of human nature in all of its manifestations and an ability to get along with people generally.
4. A comprehension of the economic, political, social, and intellectual environments of modern litigation—for cases are never tried in a vacuum.

5. The ability to reason concerning the facts, the law, the personalities involved in litigation, and the environment of a case in such a way as to solve the pending problem in the most satisfactory way possible.

6. The art of expressing one's self clearly and cogently, orally and in writing.

1. Every experienced advocate will tell you that *mastering the facts* of a case is the most difficult part of his work. There are likely to be as many different versions of the facts of a case as there are witnesses and parties in interest, and it is by no means improbable that these versions may change materially—and quite without any intentional dishonesty, such is the frailty of human memory—from the time the witnesses are first interviewed to the day of the trial. It is the lawyer's duty to know as many of these different versions of the facts as he possibly can before he comes to court, both from interviewing his own witnesses and through a pretrial examination of his adversary's witnesses, and to anticipate in his imagination those hostile versions of the facts that for one reason or another he is unable to ascertain in advance of trial. This effort to obtain a comprehensive grasp of the facts of a case from his client's point of view and to anticipate his adversary's case is seldom a routine matter; it often calls for a high degree of constructive imagination in which a knowledge of human nature that is at once broad and deep is required. This diversity of view as to the facts means that he must maintain a tentative attitude toward the facts of the case that are disclosed to him, realizing full well that at the trial he will learn things that he has never dreamed of before. By knowing or anticipating the story of each witness he will often be able to explain away seeming contradictions and thus to point up the truth. On crucial items at least he should be able to repeat the testimony of the witnesses in their own words, and on the argument of an appeal he should also be able to tell where every statement of facts appears in the record and to refer to it quickly. Such skill

rarely comes by grace; one's facilities for organizing and remembering facts must be assiduously cultivated. Fortunately,
it is his privilege—nay, his duty—to forget the facts of a case
as soon as it is over, for otherwise the advocate's mind would
become an intellectual junkyard.

Though the lawyer must know all of the facts of his case and
everybody's version of them, it is essential that he should not
harbor the notion that he is bound to tell either the trial court
or the appellate tribunal all that he knows. Indeed, there
could be no surer way of losing a case. Knowing all of the facts,
he may skillfully confine his presentation to those which are
most cogent and persuasive. His power of selection, of ar-
rangement, and of emphasis will be the measure of his genius.
He will do well to remember the force that inures in the
concrete instance in contrast to vague generalities; and he will
never forget the wisdom of Macaulay's dictum in painting a
picture to either jurors or judges: "Logicians may argue about
abstractions, but the mass of men must have images."

Not infrequently in complicated cases counsel will be called
upon almost overnight to learn about an entire art or industry
with which he may previously have been totally unfamiliar.
Thus, years ago I was called upon to defend some insurance
companies that were being sued for the loss of certain paintings which the plaintiff described as the works of certain Italian and Dutch old masters. The defense was that they were
not the old masters they were represented to be, but fraudu-
lent reproductions. The preparation and trial of the case called
for a thorough knowledge of the paintings of the Italian and
Dutch artists in question, of the characteristics and techniques
of each of them, and of the kind of canvas on which each
worked and the chemistry of the pigments each used, in contrast with the canvas and pigments disclosed by the charred
remains of the pictures that had been insured. My investiga-
tion required not only much study of books but conferences
with experts on art, canvas, and pigments, matters on which I

was blissfully ignorant before being called into the case. Every experienced trial lawyer has scores of such experiences.

2. The second element in the advocate's work, the acquisition of a thorough understanding of the fundamental *principles and rules of the law*, is one of the chief aims of every law student. To understand the law, however, in its proper perspective to the other factors in the lawyer's work, we would do well to remember that in contrast to the facts of a case, which are generally specific and concrete, the rules of law always are abstract and they deal with the relations between persons or between persons and things. It is therefore most important to form the habit of noting to one's self, throughout every step of a case and in dealing with every one of the many versions of the facts, the rules of law that apply thereto. The advocate will, of course, be interested not only in controlling rules of substantive law and the principles underlying them, but also the rules of pleading by which issues are presented in the court, and of evidence by which they are proved there. This process of applying the law, substantive and procedural, to the facts of the case is the converse of the process that the student is accustomed to use in the study of cases, but it will give him no difficulty if he has done his law school work thoroughly.

3. The third element in every lawsuit, and quite as important as the facts and the law, is the advocate's *knowledge of human nature* and his ability to get along with people. I am referring not only to the lawyer's client and his witness, but also to his adversary and his client and his witnesses, and the judge, the jury and everyone with whom he has to deal in the conduct of the suit. Each of them is a unique personality. Their variety is infinite. A single mistake in drawing a jury may cost the plaintiff his case, while at the same time a deft choice may mean victory for a defendant. "The proper study of mankind," says Pope, "is man." And for no one is this more true than for the trial lawyer. He must learn to judge character as much by a person's voice and his manner as by what he sees in his face and what he says.

It is a difficult art but a fascinating one. The prospective advocate may learn much through observation, more through conversation, but most from daily contact with people. He should school himself to make his study of human nature a lifelong habit. He may learn much through the study of the world's greatest literature, notably the Bible and Shakespeare, that he will not be able to discover elsewhere.

4. Next the advocate must know the economic, political, social, and intellectual environment of his case and the *trends of the times*. He must know whether he is working with or against what Dicey has well called "the assumptions of the age":

> There exists at any given time a body of beliefs, convictions, sentiments, accepted principles or firmly rooted prejudices, which, taken together, make up the public opinion of a particular era, or what may be called the reigning or predominant current of opinion. . . . It may be added that the whole body of beliefs existing in any given age may generally be traced to certain fundamental assumptions, which at the time, whether they be actually true or false, are believed by the mass of the world to be true with such confidence that they hardly appear to bear the character of assumptions.[1]

All this calls for a knowledge of the social sciences in the broadest sense of the term, as well as the humanities, and for insight in forecasting the trends of the future. As a profession we have been slow to recognize this responsibility. Indeed, I suspect that even you may think I am speaking not as a practical man of the law but as an erstwhile educator in urging on you desirable but not essential attainments. The matter is so vital that I cannot permit any doubt of your responsibility for preparation in this field to linger in your minds. I summon to my aid two of the greatest corporation lawyers in the country. Says Edward F. Johnson, General Counsel of the Standard Oil Company of New Jersey:

Unless the lawyer is keenly sensitive to such [social] trends, advice acted upon today is likely to fail to meet the test of judicial scrutiny years later. . . . To statute and decision has been added a new legal dimension—the dominant public interest. A lawyer's advice based upon a two-dimensional study of the law is likely to result in as great a distortion of reality and to be as flat as a two-dimensional painting without depth or perspective. A sound lawyer—sober, hardheaded and realistic craftsman that he is—pays heed to every relevant fact, whether or not that fact is to his liking.[2]

Hear also William T. Gossett, General Counsel of the Ford Motor Company:

The lawyer representing business today, if he is to live up to the challenge of his responsibilities . . . will be alive to the social, economic and political implications of the time; he will avoid a narrow, shortsighted approach to his client's problems; he will act with due regard for the social responsibilities of the enterprise; he will have the courage to advise against a business program or device which, although legally defensible, is in conflict with the basic principles of ethics. Failing this, he not only will be ignoring his obligations to society, he will be doing a disservice to his client, who may find himself in the position of winning a legal battle but losing a social war.[3]

5. The fifth factor in a lawyer's work is the *ability to reason* concerning the facts, the law, the personalities involved in litigation, and the environment of the case in such a way as to solve a controversy in the most satisfactory way possible. There is little need to talk to law students about this, for the great educational achievement of our modern law schools has been in training their students to think as lawyers think. It is the necessity of reasoning about concrete facts, abstract law, complicated personalities, and the complex social scene that

calls for such a variety of traits in the trial lawyer and that in turn makes his work so absorbing. While the lawyer thinks both inductively and deductively in preparation for trial and the courtroom, it is important to observe here that in forensic persuasion he uses largely the deductive approach.

6. Finally, the advocate must be able to *express himself* in words. He must master the use of words or they will be likely to master him. He must cultivate the arts of both written and spoken expression until their use becomes second nature to him. I do not have in mind any tricks such as sometimes masquerade under the guise of semantics. Many a case is won or lost according to the skill of counsel in translating his points into language that may be grasped by his particular audience. After he has completed his study of the facts, the law, the people of a case, and the environment, after he has exhausted his powers of reasoning, he will still have the problem of making himself so clearly and forcibly understood as to be able to persuade his hearers. They must feel—and he must be able to make them feel—that he is uttering realities and not mere words. Self-expression is, indeed, a lifelong adventure.

The law student will note that with the exception of the second factor in the advocate's work, an understanding of the law, and of the fifth, the art of legal reasoning, all of the elements that enter into his work are attributes one would expect to find in any educated and enlightened citizen. They are not narrowly professional. The more the student has learned and the more he has trained his faculties in each of these fields, the easier will be his initiation in the arts of advocacy.

All advocacy involves conflict and calls for the will to win. But the conflicts of advocacy proceed under very definite rules. The contestants must have character. This means that they have certain standards of conduct, manners, and expression that are so habitually theirs that they do not have to stop in an emergency to argue with themselves as to whether or not they should conform to them. They are free to concentrate on the task at hand. The prospective advocate may learn much from a study of the functions of the several steps in forensic persuasion, and of the different kinds of tribunals he will be called upon to address, so that here, too, in his hour of testing he will not have to stop, when his mind should be on the merits of his case, to debate with himself the intricate questions of trial or appellate tactics. He will have learned the basic rules of the contest in which he is engaging. Nothing, of course, will take the place of actual experience in developing his own skill, but a study of the problems inherent in the various phases of advocacy and of the experience of others may save him from making a multitude of unnecessary mistakes.

The advocate must also learn that hard work is his daily lot. But the reward is great. To quote Judge Cardozo, "What we give forth in effort comes back to us in character. The alchemy is inevitable." Character, capacity for hard work, the will to win, and a study of the methods of the advocate round out the requirements in preparation for the art of advocacy.

ARGUING AN APPEAL: SUBSTANCE

Coming now to a consideration of the several types of forensic persuasion, I shall first speak of the argument of an appeal, because every law student is more familiar with the work of our appellate courts from his study of reported cases than he is with any other phase of judicial activity. Even so, there is a world of difference between the student's view of an appeal and the advocate's. In your study of appellate decisions you have very largely the point of view of the appellate judge. Like the judge you are interested in ascertaining the right rule of law and the sound reason for it. The advocate, on the other hand, is bending all of his powers to persuade the appellate court to adopt a view of the facts or a rule of law favorable to his client, well knowing that his adversary will do likewise and that the judges are most likely to reach a sound conclusion if each of the rivals argues his case effectively.

The argument of an appeal is the climax of a case. All the long and wearisome work of interviewing clients and witnesses, of gathering facts, of assembling the law, of drafting the pleadings, of attending the various pretrial proceedings, the preparation of the trial briefs, the trial itself, possibly the argument of a rule to show cause why a new trial should not be granted, the preparation of the appellate briefs and of the entirely separate and distinct notes for the oral argument: all of these are to be distilled into an argument of a half an hour. It is the most concentrated and yet the most exhilarating work that the advocate is called upon to do. The trial court has had the advantage of hearing the opening and the summation of counsel, the presentation of evidence, the cross-examination of witnesses, the arguments on the admission of evidence, and perhaps a motion for a nonsuit or a directed verdict. The trial court absorbs the content of a case bit by bit. The appellate tribunal, however, will know nothing of the facts, none too much of the law, and none of the background of your case save as it gleans them from the cold pages of the printed briefs or absorbs them from counsel at the oral argument. You face a select audience that is experienced, professionally critical but not unfriendly, keenly interested in knowing the facts and applying the law to them, and more or less prepared for the occasion. The challenge is great; the entire outcome of the case, victory or defeat, will be influenced by the effectiveness of your oral argument.

There are several different methods of argument on appeal, and a brief discussion of the several kinds will throw light on the entire process. In the English appellate courts, for example, the briefs are only two or three pages long; they merely show how the case came up and list the points to be argued, but without written argument or citation of cases. The argument is entirely

oral and there is no time limit except as the judges think the
subject has been exhausted. Therefore the judges do not hesitate to interrupt counsel as frequently as they need to, to get
the facts and to express their views on the law, and counsel do
not object to such interruptions. Indeed, they welcome them
because they show what the judges are thinking and give counsel an opportunity to meet the views of the judge. Some years
ago I heard Sir William Jowitt, later Lord Chancellor, take
three days to present the facts of a very complicated appeal from
India. Everything about the man—his diction, his manners—
proclaimed him the master of the situation. Speaking entirely
without notes, only once and then upon a very minor matter did
he have to correct a statement of fact on a suggestion from his
solicitor. His tone, while conversational and reserved, left no
doubt as to the intensity of his effort and of his will to win. Each
question asked him by the court, instead of constituting a set-
back, seemed to be used by him to advance his presentation.
He gave one the impression of a swimmer who enjoyed breasting the waves and who had the knack of surmounting them.
This method of argument takes much longer than we are accustomed to, but it produces decisions that are very obviously the
joint work of court and counsel.

A series of cases in which I was interested some years ago,
each of which involved the same questions of law, took six days
in the Supreme Court of Canada, eight in the Supreme Court of
Jamaica, and the same amount of time in the Supreme Court of
Nassau, and in the Privy Council the appellant, who alone was
called on, took five days. The same issues were argued, and I
think equally thoroughly, in a half day in the United States
Court of Appeals for the Fourth Circuit with the aid of elaborate
briefs which the court had studied before the argument.

The English system does have the advantage that counsel
are always quite sure how the case will be decided before the
argument is over, and generally on what point. In the case
argued by Sir William Jowitt, I asked the registrar of the Privy

Council when the case would be decided. He told me that the judges would confer on the matter at the conclusion of the argument, which was on Friday afternoon, someone would write the opinion over the weekend, the judges would confer about it Monday morning, and I should be able to read it in the London *Times* Tuesday morning—and there it was on Tuesday morning.

In the early days of the United States Supreme Court arguments were equally long. *McCulloch* v. *Maryland* took six days, and the *Girard Will* case ten days. Unlike the English practice, questions were rarely asked by the justices. Though the time for argument was gradually lessened as the work of the Court increased, the attitude of the Court toward counsel did not change. President Nicholas Murray Butler of Columbia University used to tell of journeying to Washington at the turn of the century for the sheer delight of listening to "models of legal reasoning," as he termed the argument of counsel.

There are still courts in which the justices rarely ask questions. Chief Justice Marvin B. Rosenberry of Wisconsin delights to tell of one such court, which was visited on a hot summer afternoon by a farmer and his young son. As counsel droned on, a fly lit on the exposed brow of one of the justices and he waved it away. The fly persisted and the justice repeated his movement, whereupon the farmer's boy nudged his father and exclaimed quite excitedly, "Look, Dad, one of them is alive!"

In more recent years questions from the bench have frequently run away with the arguments in the Supreme Court of the United States. Indeed, Justice, then Professor, Frankfurter stated fifteen years ago:

The extent to which argument has become a Socratic dialogue between Court and counsel would startle the shades of Marshall and Taney even as they would have hampered the eloquence of Clay and Webster.[4]

One experience I had in which I answered thirty-two questions from a single justice in the course of an hour's argument leads me to question the soundness of the reference to Socrates, but of this more later. My discomfiture in the case I have mentioned reminds me of the story that is told in Seattle of a longshoreman who struggled to become a lawyer and finally attained his ambition of arguing a case before the United States Supreme Court. He was no sooner under way with his argument than he was beset with questions from the justice on the left end. Complaining to the Chief Justice, he said that he had worked out his argument carefully, that he could get through it in an hour if he were left alone, and therefore he pleaded with the Chief Justice to control his end men. Chief Justice Taft smilingly said that such would be the order of the day—and it was.

There are many appellate courts in which the appeals are assigned for the writing of decisions to the various justices in rotation in advance of hearing argument. Human nature being what it is, it inevitably follows that the judges who are not charged with the writing of an opinion in a particular case are not likely to take as great an interest in that case as they would if they thought they might be called on at the court conference to write the opinion. Judges in one great court have even been known to slip out for a cup of tea when a case was on in which they would not be primarily responsible for the opinion. This system, of course, is all wrong, but where it exists, counsel will do well to use all his ingenuity to ascertain who is the judge who has been assigned to write the opinion in his case. Sometimes the judge may be detected by his asking more quesions than any of the others do. Generally his law secretary will be in evidence in the courtroom, busy taking notes. In such cases counsel will, of course, give the opinion-writer more than usual attention while not seeming to neglect the rest of the bench. Where this practice of "one-judge opinions" prevails, the bar should exert its influence to end it. Such opinions are inevitably inferior to those in which the entire court really participates.

An increasing number of courts follow the example of the United States Court of Appeals for the Fourth Circuit in reading the briefs in advance of argument. In my court [the Supreme Court of New Jersey] not only do we read the briefs and as much of the record as may be necessary in advance, but each of us also prepares a typewritten summary of the points raised on the appeal and of our tentative views with respect thereto. We even go one step further; we tell counsel at the outset of the arguments the points in their briefs that we are most interested in hearing argued, but we leave it entirely to them to use their time as they see fit. The great advantage of reading the briefs first is that if there is anything in the briefs that is not clear, the judges have a chance to ask counsel about it when he reaches the point in his argument, whereas if briefs were not read until a later date that question must necessarily go unasked. There can be no doubt that any argument will be much more effective if the judges have read the briefs in advance, for in these days so great is the volume of decisions that no judge can be expected to, or does in fact, know all of the decisions of his own state. If the judges come to the oral argument fortified by a study of the briefs, the statements of counsel both as to the facts and the law have a force and a meaning they otherwise would lack. Counsel, too, have the satisfaction of knowing their briefs have been seriously studied at a time when the study will do the most good.

But whatever method of argument may be pursued in any given jurisdiction, there are four essential matters that need concern the advocate: (1) the statement of the question or questions to be argued, (2) the statement of facts, (3) the argument of law, and (4) the relation between counsel and the court, *i.e.*, between the speaker and his audience. The same four elements must be considered in preparing a brief, but the written brief, save in the rarest instances, cannot hope to move its readers. It achieves its objective if it convinces. The aim of the oral argument, however, is to persuade. The human presence and particularly the human voice can convey meanings and produce reactions, both favorable and unfavorable, far beyond the power of the printed page. More often than most counsel imagine, the oral argument may change a judge's mind, no matter how carefully he may have studied the briefs in advance. There are several reasons for this: first, ideas are developed in the clash of oral argument that never appear on the printed pages of the brief; second, many judges by reason of their years of courtroom experience get more through the ear than they do through the eye; finally, the oral argument inevitably tends to develop far better than can any brief the case as a whole in a way that delights the mind of a judge who has an instinct for order and system.

I propose to deal first with the content of the oral argument and then with the style of its presentation and finally with a variety of obstructions that often impede or defeat counsel's purpose as an advocate. But in starting I must at least indicate that though oral argument has its roots in the printed brief and counsel may refer to it frequently, the oral argument is as different from a written brief as a love song is from a novel. Counsel should never read from his brief except perhaps the shortest quotations from the most pertinent authorities. His arguments should be delivered seemingly extemporaneously, preferably with nothing intervening between the court and himself except a one-page outline of his argument, which he should keep before him so as to be sure not to skip any important point due to any interruptions from the bench. Next to reading from the printed brief itself there is nothing worse than reading ad infinitum from a sheaf of longhand notes, which gives evidence of having been prepared late the night before the argument or even on the train on the way to court. For the court the decision of an appeal is the most important type of judicial business. The judges realize they are making

law. If they are worth their salt, they are putting all they have
in experience, time, energy, and judgment into their work.
They may never tell you so, but they cannot help but resent
anything that is, or that seems to them to be, casual about
your preparation for your part of the judicial function. But
more of this also later.

In most jurisdictions a succinct statement of the question or
questions to be argued is the first element of a brief. This is to
aid the court in reading the statement of facts that follows
intelligently in the light of the issues. Yet many counsel vitiate
this requirement by obscure and verbose statements of the
questions to be argued. Why they do so is an unsolved problem of abnormal legal psychology. Even the judges who do not
read the briefs in advance of argument are likely to glance first
at the opinion of the court below and then at the statement of
the questions in each brief while counsel is warming up. If the
appellant's headings are not enlightening but the respondent's
are, whose point of view, I ask you, is likely to be uppermost
in the minds of these judges as they listen to the argument?

In those jurisdictions where the judges do study the briefs in
advance of the oral argument, many counsel seem to think that
the court reads the appellant's brief through before turning to
the respondent's. This assumes that the judges look on the
briefs as literary efforts to be digested in their entirety, but
ordinarily they do not have that point of view. They will read
first of all the appellant's statement of the questions to be
argued and then the respondent's. They do this because they
want to see whether counsel agree on the issues and if they
disagree, in what respects.

After comparing the statements of the questions to be
argued, the judges will next read the appellant's statement of
facts, following that by a study of the respondent's statement of
facts to see how far the parties agree on the facts and wherein
they differ. If necessary, the judges will look up in the record
the points of difference which they are referred to by appropri-

ate citation of pages and lines in the brief. And may a kind fate help the lawyer who neglects to cite the appropriate spots in the record to justify his statement of facts, and vainly expects the court to analyze the whole record for him in a hunt for something that it was clearly his duty to point out to the court. Worse yet is it for counsel to give an incorrect citation, either by design or mistake. But the most unpardonable offense of all is to cite a page and line of a record for a statement of fact made in the brief when no such fact appears on the cited page—when all that counsel really intended to do, or at least so he assures you at the oral argument, was to draw an inference from something that appears on the cited page without telling you that he is indulging in inference, or from what he is drawing the inference. Words of inference or reasoning are plentiful in the English language, and it is unforgiveable for counsel to draw inferences in his statement of facts without saying affirmatively that he is so doing and without telling the court from what facts he is drawing them. If counsel do not agree in their statement of the questions to be argued, the court's task in reading the statements of fact is more difficult than it would have been had they agreed, but still the judges can read each statement of fact with the differing views in mind as to the questions to be argued.

Next the court will read the appellant's argument of law one point at a time, then the respondent's response thereto, then the appellant's reply, and come to a tentative opinion on each point. If counsel understood how briefs are read—indeed, if they understood the only intelligent way in which they can be read—the briefs and the oral argument would be far different from what many of them now are. It is surprising, too, how often even the most thoroughgoing study of the briefs fails to reveal some controlling point that will be developed for the first time on oral argument, driving the court back to a rereading of the brief after the oral argument and before the court conference at which a discussion of the case will take place.

In the written briefs the statement of the issues to be argued, as we have seen, comes first, but this is not necessarily so in the oral argument. If counsel are in agreement as to the questions to be argued, as is generally the case, a preliminary statement by the appellant of the questions will give point and direction to the subsequent statement of the essential facts. If, however, counsel have not agreed in their briefs on the questions to be submitted to the court for decision, counsel will do well ordinarily to state his facts first and then to pose the questions before plunging into his arguments of the law which he contends are raised by the facts. The ideal opening for an oral argument is a plain statement in a single sentence or two of how the case came to the court, its jurisdiction over the case, and what the question or questions are to be argued.

The greatest art in the argument of an appeal lies in the statement of the facts of the case. Counsel should know every fact in all of its ramifications and be able to turn to it in the record without fumbling. Heaven forbid, however, that he should attempt in the statement of facts to tell all that he knows of what he should know! He must be able to extract from the record the relatively few facts that are significant and controlling, and to state them in language and in a manner that will capture the attention of the court. It was said of William Murray, better known as Lord Mansfield, the greatest of the English judges, that when he finished the statement of facts in a case, it seemed quite unnecessary to argue the law. Generally the facts should be summarized in chronological order. Always remember that the court does not know the facts of a case—indeed, the court is not interested in the facts except for the ephemeral purpose of deciding the case—and no effort should be spared to make sure that it has the correct view of them. Counsel will search far without finding any better example of how to present the facts of a case than may be found in some of the great opinions of Chief Justice Hughes, who both at the bar and on the bench had the rare gift of marshalling his facts so that they seemed to be marching to martial music at his direction. A study of his opinions will reveal a scarceness of adjectives and adverbs, the vitality of his verbs, and his precision in the use of prepositions and conjunctions.

Not only must counsel know every fact, all of its implications, and where to find it in the record, not only must he be able to state the pertinent facts succinctly and attractively, but he must never under any circumstances misstate a fact. And if an adversary should ever accuse him of misstating a fact, he must go to all lengths in meeting and demolishing the challenge. I had this happen to me once and I spent all but five minutes of my allotted time in answering the charge, citing page and line of the testimony. I then condensed a half-hour's argument of the law into five minutes and won my case, but I should have preferred to have lost the case than to have had the court think I had misrepresented intentionally or innocently any facts of the case or any rule of law.

Sometimes the challenge may be facetious. I remember a case in which I was representing Roger N. Baldwin, long the distinguished head of the American Civil Liberties Union, in an appeal to our former Court of Errors and Appeals on a charge of unlawful assembly. He had been convicted and his conviction had been sustained in our Supreme Court. The outlook was grim. I described how a company of silk strikers marched out from their headquarters to the City Hall Plaza in Paterson, two by two, led by two beautiful girls carrying American flags, for the purpose of reading the American Constitution there. One of the justices, who had an eye for beauty, asked me where in the record it was stated that the girls were beautiful. I told him with an air of studied innocence that I had assumed the court would take judicial notice of the fact that any girl carrying an American flag was *ipso facto* beautiful. "Quite so, quite so," he murmured. Subsequently he wrote an opinion that has become an outstanding landmark in this country on unlawful assembly.

I also remember going to see Chief Justice Gummere of the New Jersey Supreme Court on a pressing matter one summer and apologizing for interrupting him. He told me he was glad of the interruption because he had spent most of the day in the boresome work of checking item for item every statement of fact in the brief of a prominent lawyer because he didn't want to be unfair to the man's client, but he couldn't accept any statement this lawyer made without verification. All the while this particular lawyer fancied he was getting along famously with the court, though at loss to understand his more than occasional reverses.

The statement of the questions to be argued and the presentation of the facts, important though they are, are merely introductory to the argument of the law. The argument of the law of a case is the climax of an appeal. Every appellant must face up to the fact that he has failed below, either through the fault of the trial judge, the jury, or himself. He has the laboring oar and he has to row upstream, and he should frankly recognize it by the earnestness of his manner, albeit restrained by courtroom decorum. The respondent, on the other hand, is seeking a different position, at least until the appellant has had his day in court. He has won his prize below and he is merely seeking to save it.

How best can counsel argue the law of a case on the appeal? Not, as I have already said, by reading the brief, nor by quoting at great length from innumerable cases, however pertinent. Rather will he dwell on the controlling rules of law and the principles underlying these rules. In discussing any decisions cited in his brief he should summarize the facts and state the holdings concisely, giving references to the pertinent pages of his brief, but he should not quote from them, save for short, pertinent excerpts. He will also give the court the benefit of the learning of the great writers on the subject under discussion and of the Restatement of the Law when it is available, but again without lengthy quotations. His argument at its

best will move forward with logical precision and the successive steps in the development of his thesis will never be lost in
a maze of citations and quotations. While developing his own
case affirmatively, he will step by step be answering his adversary's contentions. His reasoning will always be as inseparable
from the facts of his case as are the two sides of a coin. He will
know a great deal more about the law of his case than he
possibly can hope to tell the court in the limited time allowed
for his argument. He will be as prepared to answer all questions that may be put to him on the law as he is on the facts.
Particularly will he know all of the facts of each of the cases
cited, not only in his own brief but also in his adversary's.
Nothing can be more embarrassing to counsel than to have to
admit he does not know the facts of a case he has cited in his
brief.

Counsel should hesitate to rest his case on mere technicalities, however strongly embedded they may be in earlier decisions. He should never feel safe unless he can and does demonstrate the reasonableness and the utility of the rule he is
adovcating. More and more it is becoming important to tie the
law of the case to its social environment and to show its relations to the assumptions of the age in which we live, and
counsel should be prepared to do this in telling phrases that
will serve to drive home the justice of his case.

Be brief, then, in your argument; argue rather than quote.
Stick to the facts of your case. Tie your argument to the great
underlying principles of the law. Do not neglect to demonstrate the utility of the law you are advocating. And remember
that even at its best, listening to an argument is arduous work.
Lord Denman was speaking out of a lifetime of experience
when he said: "Remember also to put forward your best points
first, for the weak ones are very liable to prejudice the good
ones if they take the lead. It would be better advice to say
never to bring them forward at all, because they are useless."[5]

What has been said about the posing of the questions to be

argued, the statement of the facts of the case, and the argument of law may have created the impression that the oral argument is simply a distillation of what appears in the brief. Nothing could be further from the truth, as becomes apparent when one adds to the picture the presence of opposing counsel and the judges on the bench. Professor George Herbert Palmer in his little masterpiece, *Self-Cultivation in English*, adjures us to "Remember the other person . . . every utterance really concerns two. Its aim is social. Its object is communication." The advocate will do well to always keep the judges in mind in arguing his appeal. It is their minds he is aiming to move, and yet he knows that there is nothing that would so quickly defeat his cause as the slightest attempt to prejudice their minds, to gloss over any of the pertinent facts of a case, or to ignore any of the earlier opinions of the court, however unfavorable they may be. Indeed, he owes the duty to the court as a matter of ethics to disclose to the court any decisions adverse to his position of which opposing counsel is apparently ignorant and yet which the court should consider in deciding the case. Some lawyers flatter themselves on their ability to appeal to what they, off the record, term the "whimseys" of the judges. I have seen this done more than once to an individual judge, nauseating though it is. That a judge permits his leg to be so pulled is presumptive proof of approaching judicial senility. I have never, however, witnessed a successful consummation of the maneuver in an appellate court, for the simple reason that such an appeal to one judge would inevitably offend everyone else on the bench.

It is much more to the point to reflect on what is going on in the minds of the judges. This you can readily do by putting yourself in the judge's place and giving thought to how you, if you were a judge, would be affected by this or that alternative presentation of the matter. Yet I dare say that this is a thought that does not by any means occur to every counsel. In thinking of what you would do if you were judge, moreover, you snould think not merely of what would be going on in your mind as you sat on the bench, but even more of what effect the argument would have on you in the discussions in the conference room and in the writing of the opinion.

It is not the glitter of the courtroom argument that counts in the ultimate decision of an appeal. When I was a law clerk, my preceptor made it possible for me to hear some great arguments. Mr. A, as I shall call him, was a great favorite of mine. He was hearty and full of wit and humor. He was pugnacious and determined. He knew all of the facts and he knew all of the cases and he told the court about them with relish. He was often opposed by Mr. B, who had no flair at all for the rough and tumble of oral argument, though he very obviously was not without a sense of humor whether the tide was running with him or against him. His delivery was jerky and his favorite gesture reminded me of nothing so much as a washwoman pushing the clothes up and down a scrubbing board. I was all for Mr. A and after each argument I so reported to my preceptor. Finally he had enough of it; he asked me one day if I hadn't followed through the decisions which had come down after each argument. Mr. A had lost them all. Mr. B had won; Mr. B's arguments had substance!

There are, of course, various types of judicial minds. Some judges are much given to standing by the existing order even where others think it has outlived its usefulness; *stare decisis* means much to them. Then again there are some judges who are much more influenced by the letter of a decision than they are by the reason that underlies it and properly controls it. Still other judges realize that the law is forever seeking to escape from the technical or irrational limitations of its earlier limited experience to a greater usefulness based upon a frank consideration of things as they actually are. Then, too, much depends on the particular field of law under review; every court is more open to new applications of old principles in certain fields of the law than in others. Thus it is generally easier to conform the law to new situations in the field of commercial transactions than it is in the law of real property, or in meeting new social conditions in the administration of criminal justice than in changing the law of trusts where the rights of beneficiaries are so frequently involved. Aside from knowing the type of judicial mind he is addressing, the more a lawyer knows of the individual judge the more persuasive his argument is likely to be, not so much by knowing what to say as what to avoid saying.

Even more fundamental than any of these considerations, and one that is all too often ignored, is the fact that until the court has read the briefs or heard the oral argument, it has not the slightest notion of the questions at issue or of the controlling facts. Indeed, we may go further and say that except in the fields in which the particular judge may have specialized, he is quite unlikely to know the law even of his own state in complete detail, though he should be expected to have grasped its general outlines and its underlying principles. Hence, the experienced advocate will not hesitate to state the questions at issue forcefully, to sketch the controlling facts in such a way that they cannot be misunderstood, or even to state his views of the law with conviction, not in any sense of 'telling the court' but simply by way of imparting to a bench of interested judges the results of his thoroughgoing study of the controlling principles of law. His argument to satisfy every type of judicial mind should run the gamut from particular rules and decisions to the statement of underlying principles and should conclude with a skillful summation of his fundamental propositions of law keyed to the pertinent facts of his case.

There is one difference between the advocate's point of view and the judge's. Unconsciously, the advocate seeks the strength to present his case effectively; the prayer of the appellate judge is for *light*—light and *not heat*. The advocate will do well to remember, too, that the longer the apprenticeship served by a judge at the bar in the trial of cases and the argument of appeals, the more likely he is to be influenced and really moved by what he hears rather than what he reads, a consideration that can only serve to inspire counsel to his best effort in the appellate court. The advocate should keep in mind at all times that judges are not usually bookish fellows who have lost touch with the actualities of life. In their work on the bench they have to deal practically with everyday problems very much as they did when they were practicing lawyers.

Counsel will do well to respect the court's antipathy to contradictions in statements of facts. They irritate the mind of the trained judge out of all proportion to their intrinsic significance. Chief Justice White is reported to have said that if a lawyer stated that an incident occurred in March and a few minutes later mentioned it as happening in May, he felt as if he had been stabbed in the mind. After such an intellectual stabbing, can the appellate judge be expected to give credence to counsel's presentation of the law? Nothing can be more damaging to an argument or to counsel's standing with the court than for him to make a statement which the subsequent examination of the case by the court will show to be untrue. On the contrary, if you have a troublesome fact in your case or if some earlier decision of the court stands in the way of your argument, it is often better to admit it frankly rather than to attempt to conceal it. You may be sure that your adversary will spare no pains to exhibit it at its worst, and frank discourse of your difficulty *may* enlist the help of the court. Lord Macmillan explained this psychological process with his customary felicity as "the instinct for rescue":

> When you know that your case is confronted with a serious difficulty in the shape of an awkward passage in the evidence or an embarrassing predicament, do not shirk it. Read the awkward passage with all emphasis or quote the authority without flinching, and point out the difficulty which it creates for you. You will almost invariably find that the first instinct of the judge is to assist you by point-

ing out that the evidence is less damaging to you than you represented or that the precedent is on examination distinguishable. The court is favourably disposed by the absence of all concealment of the difficulty and is attracted by the very statement of the difficulty to address itself to the task of solving or alleviating it. A good man struggling with adversity always makes an appeal to the judicial as well as to every other generous mind! A solution which the judge finds for a problem, too, is always much more valuable to the advocate than one which he himself offers to the Court, for the Court is naturally tenacious of its own discoveries and your opponent who ventures to challenge its solution finds his adversary not in you, but in the Court—a much more serious matter![6]

The most vexing problem in oral argument in the opinion of many lawyers is questioning from the bench. Questioning may be very helpful to counsel by revealing some difficulty a judge is having with the case and enabling counsel to resolve it when otherwise the doubt would have been carried, unanswered, into the conference room. One of the greatest difficulties that the advocate has to contend with is the judge who is always identifying the instant problem with some other case that he has had years ago, even though the two situations are not in fact at all analogous. I remember hearing the late Chief Justice Crane of the New York Court of Appeals say of one of his colleagues, "If you will grant his assumption of fact, his conclusions are irresistible." A frank question from the bench will frequently disclose some misconception of law or fact that can be speedily disposed of to great advantage. On the other hand, if the question is one on which counsel is not prepared and on which he could not reasonably be expected to be prepared, he had better say so frankly and ask leave to supply a supplemental memorandum. It is foolhardy to answer a question on oral argument if one does not know what one is talking about.

There are, however, questions from the bench that are defi-

nitely disconcerting and that serve no good purpose. Such are
the questions that would never have been asked if the judge
had read the brief. I gravely doubt the propriety of a judge
asking questions without first doing counsel the courtesy of
reading his brief, except, of course, under the English system
with their skeleton briefs and, even more to the point, no time
limits on argument. Next are the questions that admit of no
answer. In the Chicago Water Diversion litigation years ago,
Colonel J. Hamilton Lewis had just finished the arguments of
his first point and time was running against him. As he was
about to plunge into his second point, one of the distinguished
jurists remarked, "But, Colonel Lewis, I don't think I quite
understand your first point." The Colonel savagely brushed his
pink whiskers upward and forward and in his remarkably me-
tallic voice shouted, "Unfortunate, Sir, most unfortunate! My
second point is . . . " Even more subject to criticism is a running debate between counsel and a judge, for the very nature
of their positions makes the contest unequal. Finally, there are
questions, rare to be sure, where it is obvious that a judge is
definitely endeavoring to thwart counsel's argument. Even
then it is often better to suffer much rather than to make a
retort discourteous. Not all of us have the wit to reply as one
distinguished lawyer did a few years ago to a grossly improper
question from the bench of the Supreme Court of the United
States: "Your Honor, were I to attempt to answer your Hon-
or's question, it would stand for all time as a classic example of
the blind leading the blind." Questions from the bench call for
as much skill and restraint as the answers from counsel.
Rightly used, they can do much to facilitate sound decisions.

At what point should counsel answer a question of a judge?
If the question is simple, especially if it is a fact question and
can be dealt with readily without interrupting the train of the
argument, it should be answered forthwith. Such a disposition
of questions creates the best effect. On the other hand, if the
inquiry is foreign to the point he is presently arguing and he

can answer it better at a later point in his presentation, counsel should frankly say so, and then when he comes to that part of his argument he should expressly tell the judge that he is answering his earlier question. If approached in this way, the answers to questions from the bench can become the most stimulating part of the oral argument, but if counsel reflects any annoyance at being interrupted, either by voice or manner or the content of his reply, he will be doing his case unnecessary harm.

Able counsel has it within his power to curtail questions. Chief Justice Hughes, while at the bar, disliked questions. His biographer, Merlo Pusey of the *Washington Post*, has written me that his remedy was:

> . . . to present his case so clearly, so quickly, and so forcefully as to forestall any questions which might arise in the judge's mind before the question could be asked. That seems like a pretty large order, but he seems to have succeeded in many instances. Justice Cardozo told his associates on the Supreme Court that when Hughes appeared before him in New York, he always waited for twenty-four hours to make his decision to avoid being carried away by the force of Mr. Hughes' argument and personality.

Where the court is in the habit of asking questions, the advocate would do well to set aside at least a quarter, maybe more, of his allotted time for answering questions from the bench. Nothing can make counsel feel more harrassed in the argument of an appeal than to have planned a presentation using all of his allotted time only to find that the court is asking a wide variety of questions, with the result that he will either have to omit a part of his argument entirely or abbreviate each and every part of it. Above all, the appellant should reserve at least a few minutes of his time for possible rebuttal of his adversary's argument. I have never been able to understand

the ineptness of counsel who fail to do this; their helplessness
and obvious agony is a pitiable sight to behold. Counsel, moreover, need feel no compulsion to use all his allotted time or to
make a rebuttal argument, for rebuttal, like cross-examination,
may be very dangerous. To be effective it must always be brief
and on a telling point. The greatest advocates rarely exhaust
their time. When they are through they sit down, much to the
delight of the court and their waiting brethren at the bar. It is
a great mistake, as John W. Davis has well put it, for counsel
to think that he has a contract with the court to take his entire
time.

Let me conclude my discussion of the substance of an argument on appeal with a reference to the most important document in the courtroom from the standpoint of the advocate. I
refer to the one-page summary of his oral argument which he
will have in clear sight on the lectern before him whether he
needs to use it or not. It will doubtless have been written and
rewritten a dozen times as counsel has worked and reworked
each part of his oral argument to eliminate everything that is
not essential. The summary is his best safeguard that each part
of the oral argument will be treated in due proportion. Counsel will doubtless know it by heart, not from memorizing it but
from its continued rewriting and rehearsal. In addition to noting the catchwords of his chief facts and his points of argument, the summary will contain page references to any items
he may plan to quote from either the brief or the record. I
need hardly add that it will be quite different in purpose from
his brief. In its final edition it will be the capstone of his
preparation for the oral argument. On the worth of his summary will depend in very large measure the success of his
appeal. Its greatest merit is the aid that it furnishes to counsel
in readjusting his arguments to the exigencies of any situation
that develops With this map of the entire battlefield before
him, and with his forces and those of his adversary clearly
indicated, he can call up his troops in the order that best suits

his purpose. Without this means of adaptability many a cause would otherwise be lost in confusion.

ARGUING AN APPEAL: STYLE

I have endeavored to present the chief rules that must govern counsel in planning the content of his oral argument. They arise out of the nature of an appeal and the personalities of the advocate and of the judges, for experienced counsel talks only to the judges on the bench and not for the benefit of the audience, even of newspaper reporters. An acceptance of the inescapable bounds from which he must not stray in his oral argument will do much to relieve the advocate from the tension which inevitably accompanies—and very properly should accompany—his appearance in an appellate court. The more he knows and the more he respects as a matter of conscious choice the boundaries that necessarily restrict the content of his argument, and the more thorough and painstaking his preparation, the greater will be his self-confidence in the courtroom. The success of an oral argument, however, depends to a large extent on the advocate's appearance and bearing, the shades of meaning revealed by a cultivated voice and his style. Intellectual vitality and buoyancy, too, regardless of physical age, is an indispensable quality of great oral argument. Holmes has expressed the thought magnificently in speaking of Sidney Bartlett: "His manner was no less a study than his language. There was in it dramatic intensity of interest which made him seem the youngest man in the room when he spoke."[7]

In the few seconds that it takes after his case is called for the advocate to rise from the counsel table, gather his papers, approach the lectern, and utter the magic words, "May it please the Court," he will be giving the court a preview of his entire argument. If he stumbles over his chair as he leaves it, if he bundles his books and papers, his glasses and his pencil in his arms like a schoolgirl, if he waddles to the scene of action, if he puts on his glasses and then takes them off before he starts to talk, the court will know just about what it is in for. On the other hand, if he walks promptly but unostentatiously to the lectern, places all of the appellant's briefs on the right, the respondent's on the left and the single-page outline of his argument on the middle of the table before him, the court will know before the utterance of a single word that he has an orderly mind and that he knows what he wants to do with it. If he has any papers to present to the court in opening, they likewise will be arranged in orderly fashion and conformable to the practice of the court. Order is an indispensable ingredient of effective argument, and everything the advocate does and says should reflect an orderly mind.

Of course, he may fail at first for want of practice, for we are not born courtroom orators any more than we are born swimmers. From Demosthenes and Aristotle to Cicero and Quintilian, practice has been emphasized as the first law of public speaking. Several of the great chief justices of the United States are known to have practiced the delivery of their opinions before reading them in open court. Chief Justice White never felt himself equipped to present a matter for the consideration of the court in conference unless he could recite the facts of the case without referring to any papers. If these great men found practice necessary, what advocate dares to forego similar preparation?

The earlier the young lawyer begins to get used to the sound of his own voice, the better for him. If he learns how to stand; if he knows just how much volume to employ in speaking, for too much voice is quite as bad as too little; if he knows how to pace his delivery, not so slow as to weary the judges, not so fast that his thought does not sink in; if he understands the importance of emphasis, derived not necessarily from raising or lowering his voice or by increasing or decreasing its volume but by means of a simple pause, he will find that he is far less likely to be nervous than if he had to get acquainted with all of these things in the courtroom when his mind should be concentrated on the single task of transferring his argument from his mind to the minds of the judges. Forensic persuasion in an appellate court is a form of public speaking where moral earnestness and sincerity of manner command a high premium and where the slightest exhibition of artifice may destroy an argument no matter how sound its content may be. Gestures, at least planned gestures, would seem to be totally out of place. The advocate must never forget that his audience is likely to be as well versed as he in all techniques of delivery, and even more sensitive than he may be to any false note. Counsel should learn to stand up straight, balanced on his two feet, and to look the court in the eye. Nothing should come between him and the court. His summary should be in type so large that he does not need to be forever putting on and taking off his glasses to read it. One of the great objections to the reading of briefs or excerpts therefrom, or of a long argument memorandum, is that it interferes with counsel giving his entire attention to the audience that he is seeking to win.

The tone of voice that would be in keeping at a political rally or even in a large deliberative assembly is quite out of place in the appellate courtroom. The orotund quality, the accent of declamation, are as foreign to a good argument as they are to a prayer. We frequently hear it said that the ideal voice for public address is the conversational voice, but the term is likely to mislead, if not, indeed, to be entirely misunderstood. The conversational style of public address that harks back to Wendell Phillips is the ideal he must master. It is never casual or thin or unsustained, but always direct and personal. It requires no little art to talk conversationally using simple language yet with such intensity of purpose and such obvious elevation of thought as to carry with it the conviction that the speaker believes wholeheartedly what he is saying.

Always remember that there are no punctuation marks in an oral argument unless you put them there as you speak. There are no paragraphs in the courtroom unless you make your transition from one line of thought to another stand out as clearly as a pump handle. Avoid the use of such words as "former" and "latter." They are bad enough to encounter on the printed page when you can read back and discover—sometimes—what "former" and "latter" refer to, but you cannot do this when listening to a public address. You should likewise eschew at all hazards attempts at cross-references either forward or backward in your address. The judges just cannot follow you. Each sentence must stand by itself.

Much depends on a good opening. Counsel should plan and replan his first few sentences until he knows them by heart without ever having gone through the conscious process of memorizing them. If he can get his airplane off the ground in the first minute or two, the battle of delivery will be half won. Throughout the entire argument, counsel must give the impression of complete intellectual earnestness and drive, while at the same time exercising self-restraint in word and manner. This in turn will reflect itself in the tempo of his delivery. Judge Parry in his *Seven Lamps of Advocacy* gives an interesting example:

Bethell [later Lord Westbury], for instance, was a master of deliberation, remembering Bacon's maxim that "a slow speech confirmeth the memory, addeth a conceit of wisdom to the hearers." Shorthand writers listened eagerly to his speeches, fearing to miss a sentence that would ruin their report. Repetitions and unnecessary phrases were banned, and useless words he looked upon as matter in the wrong place. His voice was clear and musical, and he had a telling wit. Students from the first thronged the court to learn his magic, and judges listened to him with respect. When he was a junior it is said that Sir John Leach, the Master of the Rolls, succumbing to his arguments, said, "Mr. Bethell, you understand the matter as you understand everything else." And that was the real secret of Mr. Bethell's eloquence.[8]

The time will undoubtedly come when his mind will play a trick on the advocate and for a moment he will not have the slightest idea of what he has been saying or what he wants to say next. There is an interesting passage in the autobiography of Andrew D. White, the great president of Cornell University, in which he tells how President Tappan of the University of Michigan advised him as a young professor, when he confessed his trepidation at delivering his first extemporaneous lecture, "Never stop dead; keep saying something." The summary of your argument, which is the only paper spread before you on the lectern, will quickly help you out of any such temporary embarrassment.

Another difficulty that frequently afflicts public speakers is the embarrassment of getting so snarled up in the involutions of a series of complex and compound clauses that they cannot find their way out of the labyrinth of a sentence they have constructed. This will never disturb an experienced speaker. He will break off when he is lost in the maze of his own words, saying, "In short," and then summarize his thought in a very brief and telling simple sentence. Let me quote Professor Palmer again:

Of Patrick Henry, the orator who more than any other could craze our Revolutionary fathers, it was said that he was accustomed to throw himself headlong into the middle of a sentence, trusting to God Almighty to get him out. So must we speak. We must not, before beginning a sentence, decide what the end shall be; for if we do, nobody will care to hear that end.[9]

Nor should the speaker be too much disturbed if occasionally he finds himself giving voice to sentences with plural subjects and singular verbs or *vice versa*. The thought is paramount; grammar a mere means to an end.

The speaker will be helped much by a proper attitude toward the court. Too much respect is as bad as too little. Your attitude should be one of restrained decorum. The seats on the bench are, or should be, arranged at such a level that you can look the court in the eye, looking neither up nor down. Counsel will do well to seem to address the entire court, while at the same time keeping his eye on the center of the bench. Sooner or later you will be attracted instinctively to some one particular judge without anyone knowing that you are addressing him especially, least of all the judge himself. You will find yourself preparing your argument with him in mind and observing the effect of your argument on him. I did this for a quarter of a century, and I doubt that the particular judge ever knew that I had any special interest in him, for he lived in another part of the state and I am sure that I never had a hundred words of conversation with him in his lifetime. But somehow or other he did write a considerable number of opinions in the cases in which I prevailed.

Listening to oral argument five hours a day is hard work even if you have read the briefs in advance. Accordingly, if you can give the court a fraction of an excuse for a passing smile, without, of course, seeming to lug your humor in, you will be doing your cause no harm. But woe betide you if your effort does not appear spontaneous! Remember, however, that it will do you no good to become known as a professional humorist.

I have been speaking chiefly of the physical aspects of style in oral argument, first, because these are matters which seem most to concern the novice, and, second, because they are matters concerning which there can be no dispute as to the objectives to be sought and little room for argument as to the means of attaining them. When we turn to style in the sense of diction, we are dealing with larger considerations. "Style," the rhetoricians grandly tell us, "is the man." Whatever may be the truth of this statement generally, with respect to oral argument style is, first of all, the subject matter of the argument; next, the judges to whom it is addressed; and finally, the lawyer who is making the argument. What might be entirely suitable diction in the appeal of a conviction for murder would be entirely out of place in the argument of the constitutionality of a tax structure. There is as much variety in courts as there is subject matter. Adaptability to the subject matter and to the court stands foremost among the requisites of style. The supreme test of diction in oral argument is whether it pours forth extemporaneously or seemingly so, and whether the advocate creates the impression that he is talking realities that become lodged in the consciousness of his hearers rather than mere words or propositions of law for the judges to dissect calmly.

Of one thing we may be very sure, and that is, although the advocate may be inspired by his cause and stimulated by the judges he is addressing, no oral argument can be greater than the person who is making it. His knowledge of the facts, his comprehension of the law, his grasp of human nature, his understanding of the assumptions of the age, his power of reasoning, his knowledge of the wellsprings of literature, his skill in the choice of diction, his moral character, and his passion for justice set the limits beyond which his oral argument cannot hope to go.

ARGUING AN APPEAL: OBSTRUCTIONS

It would be pleasant if one might tell the future advocate that the best way to get started on his career would be to go to court and listen to the argument of appeals. Unfortunately he would be more likely to acquire bad habits from what he sees and hears than good, for it cannot be gainsaid that, whatever may be said of the exceptional lawyer, in general lawyers' skill

in oral argument has fallen over the last half century. It may
be helpful, even though it may seem like constructing a chamber of horrors, to point out some of the more common obstructions that get between the advocate and the court.

Counsel should give some thought to how he affects the eye
of the court. He would do well to remember that most judges,
regardless of what their politics may be, are a bit conservative
in matters of dress. The court sees counsel before it hears him.
If he is dressed for the race track rather than the courtroom,
the judges will form an impression that even a silver voice and
the concourse of sweet sounds may never be able to blot out.
Gone are the days of formal dress except for government offi-
cials in the United States Supreme Court, but counsel everywhere will still do well not to attire themselves in such manner
as to direct the attention of the court away from their argument to their apparel.

Counsel should avoid what is technically called the quarter-
back eye, the habit of glancing up and down the bench as if
looking for an opening in the enemy's line where he might
break through for a touchdown. Another disturbance to the
eye of the court, and hence an obstruction to counsel's argument, is the annoying habit some advocates have of waving a
pencil at the court as if they were conducting an orchestra, at a
moment perhaps when the court is endeavoring to concentrate
on some intricacies of unfamiliar facts or a complicated question of law. There is another species of amateur advocate who
poises his pencil in midair, generally in the line of vision, as if
he were able to perform some feat of mental arithmetic.
Pencil-poising stamps the offender as an office lawyer, most
likely a conveyancer, who is out of his element in the courtroom. There is, of course, nothing that compels counsel to
make such a confession to the court and he would be much
better off if he would keep his pencil in his pocket.

Counsel should respect the ear of the court as well as the
eye. Do not pound the lectern, especially when a glance at the

bench discloses that not a single justice is slumbering. Do not speak in an angry voice no matter what the provocation. There is no record of any appeal having been won by being ill-tempered. Nor does it ever pay to attack the trial judge whose opinion is being reviewed. I have heard counsel start his argument by saying, "This is an appeal from a judgment by Judge A, but there are numerous other good reasons for reversal." This is good for a smile from the lawyers in the courtroom or maybe from the court, but it never pays. Reviewing courts in particular dislike personalities. They have their own way of taking care of blundering trial judges, if counsel by his ineptness does not make it impossible. I remember a case in which I argued the appeal where the court below had done almost everything that it should not have done. In the first draft of my brief I dealt with the trial judge without mercy, but in my second draft and in my oral argument I treated the offender with urbane respect. My restraint was rewarded with an opinion of reversal which started: "The case is so curiously replete with error that our only difficulty is to decide on what ground we ought to put the necessary reversal." Then followed several paragraphs, each stating a ground of reversal, and the opinion concluded: "We must not be understood by our silence to express toleration of the other defects in the plaintiff's case."[10]

A week or two after his opinion came down, the judge who wrote it congratulated me on my restraint in not criticizing the trial judge, remarking that had I done so it would have made it impossible for him to rebuke the trial judge in his opinion. Nor is it wise to attack your adversary personally. Dwell on the facts rather than indulging in characterizations; and if the facts warrant condemnation, you may be sure that the court will administer it.

Do not toady to the individual judges. When you cite a case that one of the justices decided, you do not need to tell him that he wrote the opinion. He is either proud of the opinion or with the passage of time ashamed of it. If he is proud of it, he will assume that everybody on the court knows it; and if he is a bit ashamed of it as an early effort, he would prefer not to be reminded of it. Think, moreover, of the other justices who are not thus singled out for distinction. Above all, do not tell a judge that his opinion is a great landmark. Nor is it necessary or permissible to thank the judges for listening to your argument. It is their duty to do so.

On the other hand, there is little to be gained from needlessly offending the court. Only a few weeks ago counsel in all seriousness assured us that the decedent was an "infirm, old woman sixty years of age." He seemed quite embarrassed when one of my colleagues reminded him that the average age of the court he was addressing was well over sixty! Few of us would think it advisable to emulate Daniel Webster, who in the course of an argument in the United States Supreme Court paid his respects to the entire bench:

> No one of the judges who were here then now remains. It has been my duty to pass upon the question of the confirmation of every member of the bench; and I may say that I treated your honors with entire impartiality, for I voted against every one of you![11]

Counsel will be well advised not to do anything that will cast the slightest doubt on the thoroughness and the intensity of his preparation. What can the court think of a lawyer who requests permission to add to his brief some cases that he has discovered since the brief was written, when the cases in question have been in the books for many a year? Of course, decisions that have come down since the printing of the brief stand on a different footing.

I cannot understand why counsel, no matter how hard pressed, should ever say to the court, "I didn't try the case below," or still worse, "I didn't prepare the brief." There is no better way to put a curse on your appeal. Whether or not you tried the case or prepared the brief, you are arguing it and you must assume the responsibility for it. It is a sign of weakness for counsel to submit to coaching from his associates during his argument. The notes which are passed up to counsel by his associates in the course of an argument seem always to be either illegible or unintelligible. They require counsel to interrupt his argument to try to find out what they mean. They inevitably distract his mind from his argument and they are always the equivalent of one's junior saying to the court that the speaker is either not prepared or that he is incompetent to make the argument unaided. One great advocate I knew issued binding instructions to his associates never to come to his aid unless he should pass out in a faint and then not to do so if the court was watching! Counsel should avoid telling the court that he is sincere about what he is saying. If his sincerity does not penetrate to the court through what he is saying and the way he is saying it, the bare assertion of his sincerity will only serve to cast further doubt on it.

I have dwelt on the argument of an appeal not only because it is most closely related to the kind of legal material with which you are most familiar as law students but also because, by and large, it is typical of all forensic persuasion. If you can argue an appeal well, there is no reason why you cannot open a case and sum it up well, or argue a motion for a nonsuit or for a directed verdict, or a motion for a new trial, or the various motions directd to the evidence in the course of a trial. Whatever difficulties you may encounter are due solely to differences in the tribunal addressed or the immediate purpose at hand. The essentials are similar in every instance.

OPENING A CASE

The opening of a case to a judge or to a judge and jury is a matter of great importance to the outcome of the litigation. The opening is the picture which you present to the court or jury to give them a preview of your case before they listen to the evidence. What they get out of the evidence you will introduce will depend in large measure on the skill with which you have prepared them for it through the picture of your case. Your opening will set the pitch and the tempo of your part of the trial. Making an opening, therefore, is no mere matter of form but constitutes an art of very real importance.

Openings are of two kinds, one to a judge sitting alone and passing on both the law and the facts, the other to a judge and a jury with the judge as the arbiter of the law and the jury as the trier of the facts. In opening a case to a judge sitting alone it is important to know whether he has read the pleadings, whether there has been a pretrial conference at which the issues in the case have been simplified by him for purposes of trial, and whether he has read your trial brief. If he has, he is likely to suggest that you waive an opening, but if you can open the case without, of course, going against his instructions, it is highly advisable to do so; first, because many judges get things through the ear better than they do through the eye; second, because even if he has read the pleadings, the pretrial confer- ence order, and the trial briefs, there is a definite advantage in being able to summarize them at the outset of the trial; and finally, because it will be helpful to your client and your wit- nesses if they can see your entire case in perspective before they testify. One way or another, it is as essential that the judge have a preview of the facts as it is for the jury. In opening to a judge it is permissible and often desirable to state the issues of law as well as the issues of fact to be tried so that he will have the entire situation before him. In opening to a jury, however, counsel will rarely have occasion to deal with problems of law for those are for the court; he will ordinarily confine his atten- tion to a presentation of the facts of the controversy.

Trial judges differ from each other quite as much as appel- late judges do, and jurors are infinite in their variety. The advocate's problem is, therefore, one of adapting his tactics in the particular case to the characteristics of the tribunal he is addressing. However much the judges and jurors may differ, there are certain general principles concerning an opening that have as much force as if they were written law. Start by identifying the parties and their respective counsel. In the ordinary case the opening should be brief and simple. It should be a statement of what you expect to prove. Generally it is a mistake to go into detail or to narrate what you expect each witness to tell. Your audience will get lost in details, and besides, your witnesses may not say what you expect them to say on the stand. Stick to essentials. Emphasize the elements of liability and the ingredients of your claim for damages. While explaining your case to the judge or jury give them the drama of the litigation and endeavor to arouse their interest in your side, without, of course, any direct appeal. Let the facts tell the story. It is always wise to understand what one hopes to prove. The jurors have a way of remembering what counsel said he was going to demonstrate, and if he fails to do so they are likely to hold it against him and his client. It is far better to let the judge and the jury discover for themselves interesting things in your case, once you have aroused their interest and sympathy, rather than to endeavor to tell them everything. What they discover for themselves they are most likely to remember, when they come to decide the case.

Summarize and suggest evidence, therefore, rather than recount it at length. Do not, however, make the jury guess what your proof is going to be. Above all things, be sure that you tell the jury enough to make out a prima facie case, otherwise you may be in danger of having your adversary move for a nonsuit on your opening and succeed on his motion. Ordinarily the best way to present the facts of a case is in chronological order. Strive for continuity. In any event, it is important that the judge and the jury see that you have a plan and order above your presentation. Nothing so wearies a tribunal as to have to skip backward and forward in their case. Nothing could be more likely to cause them to lose faith in you and your cause.

There are few cases in which there is not some fact or some witness that counsel wishes he could get along without, but which, nevertheless, is there and must be recognized. It is better to be frank with the jury about these matters, though, of course, without emphasizing them. If you must rely on a witness with a shady past or a criminal record, mention it casually, minimize it if you will, but do not let it come later in the case as a surprise. If there is a letter that should not have been written but which cannot be ignored, mention it and tell the jury that you will explain it and how. On the other hand, an opening is no place for an argument. That is the function of your summation. Not only should counsel not argue in his opening, but he should avoid any statement that can call for proper objection from his adversary. Nothing will so wreck an opening as legitimate interruption by opposing counsel. Do not, therefore, refer in your opening to evidence that you know will be held inadmissible later on in the trial, because counsel will most surely object, break the thread of your opening and give you a bad start with the jury.

Either side may waive an opening but it is never advisable to do so. It creates a bad impression. The jurors will think either that you have something you don't want to tell them, that you prefer to play poker until the evidence is all in, or that you think the case is not important enough to explain to them. In any event, they will feel cheated and they will not like it.

Always take notes of your adversary's opening so that you can quote in your summation anything that he says in his opening he will prove but fails to. It is not that you will not remember what he said in his opening, but it always impresses the jury for you to appear to have his exact words on crucial points available in written form.

The opening should not be a humdrum affair. It should create a sense of expectation on the part of the jury. Everything I have said about style and delivery and obstructions in the argument of an appeal applies with equal, if not even greater, force in a trial court. Don't read anything to the jury if you can avoid it. Paraphrase a document rather than read it. Don't let anything get between you and the jury except, if you need it, your one-page outline of your opening. Do not rant or rail either in an opening or a summation. Let your language be simple, your manner direct.

Max Steuer, who was one of the greatest jury lawyers of his day, habitually spoke so softly to the jury that very often the judge and opposing counsel had to ask him to raise his voice so that they could hear what was going on between him and the jury. This method may not give you a great reputation as a jury orator, but if you are as interested as your client presumably is in the verdict I commend it to you. Mr. Steuer was so careful of the effect of little things on the jury that he never carried a leather briefcase for fear that the jury would get a wrong notion of him. He kept all his papers in a simple large filing envelope—a detail, if you please, but it points up what I have been saying about not letting anything get between you and your jurors. Mr. Steuer never let anyone sit at the counsel table with him and he was happy when opposed by a half a dozen lawyers. He would play David, they Goliath.

Do not pound the rail of the jury box. The story is told of a trial lawyer who was so annoyed at his adversary's doing so that he told the judge his adversary had reminded him of something he had omitted to do in his address to the jury. He asked for permission to take care of it. He advanced to the jury box and thumped the jury rail three resounding whacks and then sat down. The jury got the point; his adversary's speech had been demolished.

Finally, do not lecture the jury. Treat them with the same respect that you would treat an appellate court. Indicate that you have confidence in their honesty, their intelligence and their practicality. Then sit down.

SUMMATION

Summations, like openings, are of two sorts. A summation to a judge sitting alone is quite different from a summation to a jury. It is very much like the argument of an appeal with the exception that it is before a single judge instead of a bench of judges, and also that the judge has just heard the evidence and it is fresh in his mind as it has developed during the trial. With these exceptions taken into account, everything that has been said about the argument of an appeal would apply with equal force to a summation before a trial judge. The facts are to be marshalled in orderly fashion from your client's point of view and the rules of law applicable thereto should be presented as clearly and cogently as possible. In dealing with the facts and likewise with the law, counsel should make proper use of what he has learned is going on in the judge's mind from the judge's remarks and his attitude as the trial progressed. Counsel has had a preview of the judge's mind, which should help him in deciding both what to say and what not to say. There is, of course, the chance that the judge may change his mind in the final moments of the trial, but the chances are against it. Any questions from the bench during the course of the summation should be quickly, tersely and frankly answered. They are entitled to a weight that does not attach to the questions of any one appellate judge; they are obstructions in the path of your victory; and quite literally they must be disposed of before counsel may safely proceed. If a one-page summary of one's argument is helpful on appeal, it is doubly helpful in summation before a trial judge in organizing one's thoughts on the facts and on the law. Simplicity and clarity are quite as important as in any argument before a jury.

Quite as much as with a jury, no result is ever impossible in summation to a judge. Let me give an illustration from my own experience. One afternoon as I was returning from an argument in our Supreme Court I found a client waiting for me at the railroad station. He was the head of a large tool manufacturing concern and at the time we were in the midst of World War I. He told me that one of his most important foremen had been arrested the day before, charged with driving his automobile while intoxicated, and that he was going on trial before a local justice of the peace that evening. I suggested that we interview the foreman, but my friend said that would be useless, that not only had he been happily drunk but he had driven his car several times up over the sidewalk for the sheer joy of frightening people, though he had not injured anyone. I inquired about the judge and my client told me that he was a retired school teacher, a man of probity, very strict and fond of reading *The Lives of the Chief Justices*, to whom, it was suspected, he saw some slight resemblance in himself. The offense carried with it a minimum mandatory jail sentence of thirty days. The prospect was not alluring, especially as the foreman had picked out a Sunday morning right after the close of church services when people were on their way home from divine worship to try his sidewalk jumping. And the foreman had a name that was decidedly Teutonic.

The justice of the peace usually held court in his kitchen, but in this instance the audience was so large that he had a table brought into his garden and set up there. I shall not attempt to tell you how many witnesses testified to the foreman's antics. Fortunately, none of them seemed to bear him any ill will. His previous conduct had been exemplary. They all commented on his character and his good nature. There was little evidence I could offer beyond his record of hard work for long hours seven days a week for many months in the war effort and the fact that he had three sons at the front.

With the evidence all in, the justice asked me if I had anything to say, with the accent significantly on the word "anything." Without stressing my words too much, I said that I had no intention of attempting a jury speech which I knew in the circumstances and with his reputation would be unavailing, but

I did want to point out some significant facts. First of all, the charge was driving an automobile while intoxicated. True, several witnesses had testified that the defendant was drunk, very drunk, in fact, but not disagreeable and malicious, just happy and carefree; but he had been a good family man with a fine record up to the time of the present charge, and his services were much more needed in the factory superintending the production of war tools than they were in the county jail repenting his folly. Once more I managed to bring the word 'intoxication' in the complaint in contrast with the word 'drunk' in the testimony, but I made no effort to press the distinction. I noticed however, a glint in the judge's eye, whether friendly or not I could not fathom, as I continued with my general remarks on the state of affairs in the factory, in the world at large and with families divided, the flower of youth doing their duty all over the globe. The foreman's two daughters fell to weeping silently and before long most of the women in the audience were teary-eyed and more than one grown man was busy blowing his nose. I reminded the judge of his hard responsibility and wished that I could suggest some way out of the dilemma, but I realized that he was sworn to do his duty and I was no man to dissuade him, but where there's a will there's a way and the world was tumbling all about us.

When I concluded, the judge went into his kitchen and came out with a copy of the Revised Statutes, which he opened ostentatiously. He read the section that the defendant had offended. He reviewed the evidence, I must say, with great effect to the accompaniment of tears from the feminine part of his audience. He commented on the danger to the public resulting from the defendant's conduct. He spoke, too, of the great strain that the defendant had been under and the service that he had been rendering his country as well as of the courage of his sons. He then referred again to the statute book and called attention to the fact that the charge was driving while intoxicated and he then laid great stress on the fact that while the many witnesses had testified that the defendant was drunk, not a single one had testified that he was intoxicated. Therefore he had no choice but to acquit the defendant, but in doing so he warned him that the next time he was drunk someone would possibly be found who would testify that he was intoxicated. I bowed in due respect to the judge's wisdom and he received the thanks of the defendant, his wife, his daughters and his friends, who seemed all of a sudden to make up the entire audience. Nobody doubted that in the circumstances justice had been done, whatever might be said of the judge's canons of statutory construction.

One of the most troublesome aspects of summation to a single judge is met when he becomes interested in reading a pleading or a trial brief or a judicial decision during the course of your argument or when he is interrupted by one of the court officers with some message. If the interruption promises to be a short one, counsel had better continue as if nothing had occurred. If the interruption continues, there is nothing to do but to take the risk of offending the judge by stopping short in your speech until you have regained his attention. Quite different is the judicial habit of shutting one's eyes. This does not always portend slumber. I recall visiting in the Court of Appeals of the Province of Ontario not so long ago and seeing a judge with his eyes shut and his head curled up on his left shoulder and his arms folded. I wrote a note to my guide and asked who the little brown bear was who seemed to be hibernating on right end. A note written in reply told me the little brown bear was Mr. Justice Middleton but that he was not hibernating, as I should see presently. Within three or four minutes he unfolded his arms, opened his eyes and asked counsel if he was acquainted with such and such a case. Counsel confessed that he was not and then the judge suggested that they take a look at it. Presently counsel was admitting that the case was in point and seemed to state him out of court, whereupon the judge kindly said that he should not feel too

bad because unfortunately the case had not been properly
digested or indexed and so counsel should not be expected to
know about it.

A fine summation to a jury is a dramatic event. Mr. Justice
Holmes has painted the type; speaking of George Shattuck he
said:

> He was a great man with the jury in every way. His
> addresses carried everything before them like a victorious
> cavalry charge, sometimes, it seemed to me, sweeping the
> judge along with the rest of the rout.[12]

The facts will necessarily predominate. Ordinarily the law will
be given to the jury by the court, or in some jurisdictions has
been given to the jury before counsel starts his address. It is
the facts, then, that demand the advocate's attention. Not only
the facts but all of the reasonable inferences and deductions
and conclusions which may be drawn from them are counsel's
province. The effective organization of one's material, clarity,
force, and sincerity are the paramount considerations. Make
the most of the opening minutes of your address to the jurors,
for then they are most attentive and most receptive. Next in
importance to the opening of your speech is the conclusion,
provided, of course, you haven't lost their attention in the
meantime. If you see the attention of the jury flagging and you
can't revive it, get to the end of your remarks no matter how
much more allotted time you may have.

Do not go outside of the record in your summation, for otherwise opposing counsel will have just cause to interrupt you and
your address will be spoiled. Organize the facts and present
them succinctly. Generally the chronological order is best.
Make only such deductions and inferences from the testimony
as will appeal to the intelligence of the jury. If you are far-
fetched in your reasoning, you will be sure to draw down on
your head the ridicule of your adversary. Be reasonable. In

many instances the inferences that may be drawn from the testimony are far more important than the testimony itself. I recall a case where the plaintiff and several of his employees did not take the stand, though they could have given evidence to rebut much of the defendant's proof. The defendant's counsel in summation took about ten minutes to summarize his defense, and then spent the rest of the time telling the jury what the plaintiff and his employees could have proved had they been on the stand and then taunted the plaintiff's attorney to tell why he did not put them on the stand. The plaintiff's attorney saw that he had to explain his failure to do so and used up all his time in doing so and never got around to summarizing his own case, with the inevitable result that he lost the verdict.

Regardless of what the technical rules of law may be, every argument to the jury, to be effective, must appeal to the jury's concept of essential fairness and justice. Juries are rarely interested in technicalities. Ordinarily the fewer points the jury is called upon to deal with in the summation, the better. It is likely to be fatal if one scatters one's fire in too many directions on a multitude of points. On the other hand, although it is unwise to develop too many points in a summation, it is well to remember that there are twelve different minds on the jury and it is better to appeal to more than one type by more than one different argument. Take a middle ground. Develop a few of your strongest points. And in the course of developing your strongest points you must at the same time make sure to point out the weaknesses of the defendant's side.

An advocate must be able to say with Montague Williams: "I am by trade a reader of faces and minds," and if you find that you are losing the interest of the jurors on one front you should seek at once to arouse it on another. To have control of your case you should have an outline of your summation either in mind or on a single page, just as the advocate does on the argument of an appeal. If you can find a telling slogan or catch phrase that the jury may leave the courtroom remembering, so much the better. Don't read to the jury any more than you can avoid. There may be lawyers who can read well to a jury, but I have never heard one. There is one exception: when you come to the crucial parts of the case, very real advantage may be had in quoting briefly from your notes of counsel's opening or a vital line from a witness's testimony, but not too much, of course. Just a word or two to show that your opponent has misstated or overstated his case in his opening, just a line or two from the testimony to show exactly what it was that an all-important witness had to say, may well prove decisive. On the other hand, never memorize a summation. The course of events at the trial may force you to change your plan of attack or of defense and with a memorized speech this is indeed difficult. The odds are all in favor of a lawyer with a good clear outline from which he can vary as necessity demands. All your effort should be devoted to persuading the jury that the facts and the law are on your side and that justice and honesty will prevail if their verdict is in your favor; otherwise they are not likely to decide for your client, however eloquent you may be.

Though one may never thank a judge for listening, it is permissible and generally advisable to thank the jury, not obsequiously but courteously and briefly, for their attention. In appropriate cases one will do well to impress the jury with the importance of their power. Put the burden of the decision on the jurors' souls. Speaking of a case where Marshall Hall did just this for twenty minutes without touching upon a single fact of the case, Solicitor General Melville said: "After twenty minutes of dispassionate and pulverizing rhetoric the jury were in a state of pulp."[13] It is no wonder, then, that one of their number was physically overcome and actually fainted. Such appeals, must, of course, be reserved for cases of grave importance or they would seem ridiculous, but the thought of the importance of the jury's function should never be out of counsel's mind in any case, however restrained his effort may be in the circumstances of the case.

In dealing, with adverse witnesses who clearly have not told the truth, it is generally better to treat them as if they had made a mistake rather than as if they were deliberate perjurers. The sympathy of the jury is apt to be with the witness rather than with the advocate who has exposed him. It is only in those cases where the perjury is beyond the shadow of a doubt that it is safe to attempt to destroy the witness and not merely his testimony.

It is equally important not to indulge in far-fetched inferences from the testimony or in any kind of extravagant claims. If you represent the defendant, your opponent coming after you will surely explode your rhetoric. Even if you are speaking last, remember that the jury thinks better of an argument that is reasonable and clear. Above all jurors insist on sincerity—they are likely to favor the lawyer who seems to subordinate himself to his cause and who is giving everything within his power. Such a lawyer is likely to win the confidence of the jury without being in the least familiar with them. Courtesy, clearness, common sense, fairness, and moral earnestness should mark the progress of a summation to its conclusion. As long as human nature is what it is, true eloquence springing from the mind and the heart of the speaker will be a factor to be reckoned with in any courtroom and at no time more than in summation.

One final word: young lawyers are much concerned over their nervousness in public address and especially in summations. They should know that every speaker worth listening to is nervous, nervous about his equipment, his preparation, his audience, the hundred and one things that may go wrong. It may interest you to know that as great a speaker as Woodrow Wilson never made an address without his knees shaking for five or ten minutes. The sensitivity to an audience is one of the marks of the great speaker. A speaker who lacks this quality cannot hold an audience. The remedy is the understanding of the conditions of the particular address you are called upon to deliver, thorough preparation, and experience. You must learn to make your nervousness work for you.

MOTIONS ON THE EVIDENCE IN THE COURSE OF A TRIAL

In every trial there is sooner or later a clash over the admission of evidence. Prepare oneself as one will on both the substantive law of the case and on the law of evidence, there are still many aspects of such clashes that cannot be worked out in advance. One's presentation therefore has to be extemporaneous and calls for presence of mind in high degree. To be effective, one's presentation of the issue of fact or law or both must combine brevity and clarity. Wit and good humor are helpful, but there are many occasions that call for the exercise of all the willpower at counsel's command. If the question is crucial—and I am not, of course, referring to the scores of useless objections that have a way of intruding themselves into the trials conducted by pettifoggers—one simply must win then and there, or go through the pains of a long trial on a wrong basis, often with disastrous results. Too much attention, therefore, cannot be paid to, and too much effort cannot be expended in preparation for these encounters. The rules are simple, though the execution be difficult: be prepared, be clear, be as brief as possible, but be tenacious. Tie the particular question to the larger issues of the case, and fight—courteously, of course, but with all the resources of intellect and will at your command.

An even greater difficulty than those encountered over the admission of evidence will sooner or later overtake counsel in his courtroom work, and that is a clash with the court. I recall an equity suit where opposing counsel had failed to break a witness's story on cross-examination and the court, evidently being of the opinion that the witness was not telling the truth, took over the cross-examination, but equally without success. After a long cross-examination, the judge said, "Let the record show that this witness's answers have been in a low and almost inaudible voice and most hesitatingly." Now, in an appeal from a judge sitting alone the reviewing tribunal naturally gives great heed to the impressions of the trial judge as to the veracity of the witness. With that remark unchallenged in the record the reviewing court would be likely to sustain almost any construction that the trial judge might place on the witness's testimony. Much as I disliked to quarrel with the court, I had no choice but to state to the court that if the court's remark stayed on the record, "I think in fairness it ought to be stated that the witness's answers on direct examination were given in the same tone of voice and in the same deliberating manner," to which the court reluctantly replied, "Yes, of course." But even this admission would not have cured the harm which had been done on the record, so I had to add, "And that he looked his examiner in the eye throughout his testimony, because I think that is just as apparent as the fact that he speaks in a low voice, and that he never flinched," to which the court replied even more reluctantly, "That may also appear on the record." These encounters are unpleasant, but counsel will be failing in his duty to his client and to the court in the administration of justice if he does not stand up in such cases. In the long run the judges will respect him for his courage and admire him for his courtesy.

Sooner, or later, too, you will meet up with a judicial bully; a species never quite extinct. Some day a judge in the heat of courtroom controversy will tell you to sit down when you stand up to make an objection. My advice in such circumstances is to decline to do it. On the contrary, you should stand on tiptoe just to look a little bit taller than ever. If counsel ever surrenders to a bullying judge, the jury will lose all respect for him. Questions from the bench to the witness on either direct or cross-examination should be treated pre-

cisely as if they came from opposing counsel. It is not pleasant
to have to object to a question from the court and then to have
the court rule on its own question, but if the question is improper it is counsel's duty to do so, no matter what the immediate consequences may be. Ordinarily the jury will understand, and in any event you will keep your self-respect, which
is indispensable.

There probably never has been an advocate who equaled
F.E. Smith, later Lord Chancellor Birkenhead, in the art of
dealing with either the court or opposing counsel. I cannot
refrain from quoting three samples of his skill: first, in dispos-
ing of an adversary, second, in setting straight a talkative but
not unfriendly judge, and third, in putting in his proper place
an unfriendly jurist. They are all masterpieces of forensic give-
and-take that will be hard to match:

> Despite his reputation as a witty and ruthless cross-
> examiner, Smith made it a rule never to score off counsel
> on the other side except in self-defense. If the other bar-
> rister did not interfere with him, Smith left him alone.
> But if the other barrister began a personal conflict, he
> regretted it. On one occasion Smith found himself op-
> posed by the late Sir Patrick Rose-Innes, a florid and
> somewhat pompous K.C., who had taken silk after forty
> years at the Junior Bar. Smith, in his speech to the jury,
> referred to Innes' client as "this old scoundrel." "I deter-
> mined," Innes related afterwards to a friend, "to shut
> F.E. up. I rose, and F.E. sat down. 'M'Lud,' I said to the
> judge, 'my client is a merchant in the city of London. I
> submit that it is most improper to refer to him as "this old
> scoundrel." ' Smith got up again when I sat down, and
> addressing the jury again, said: 'As I was saying, this *frau-*
> *dulent* old scoundrel . . .' I didn't dare to interrupt him
> again, because I didn't know what adjective would come
> next."

Another good story told of him concerns his opening a
case before Mr. Justice Ridley, of whom it may be said

that, whatever his merits, he is not the most judicial person who has adorned the Bench. When Smith rose to address the jury, the judge made this remarkable observation: "Mr. Smith, I have read the pleadings, and I do not think much of your case." "Indeed, m'Lud, I'm sorry to hear that" was the instant reply. "but your Lordship will find that the more you hear it, the more it will grow on you!" The judge burst into a roar of laughter, and Smith, duly addressing the jury, won his case.

He appeared one day for a tramway company sued for damages for injuries caused to a boy who had been run over. The plaintiff's counsel pitifully explained that the boy had gone blind as a result of the accident. "Blind? Poor boy!" said the judge, Judge Willis, much affected; "stand him on a chair, and let the jury see him!" This extraordinary unjudicial suggestion roused Smith's wrath. "Perhaps," he suggested icily, "Your Honor would like to pass him round the jury-box." "That is a most improper observation," said the judge. "It was provoked," retorted Smith, "by a most improper suggestion." The judge was furious. "Mr. Smith," he cried, "you remind me of a saying by Bacon, the great Bacon, that 'youth and discretion are ill-wedded companions.'" Now Smith had had up his sleeve for years one of Bacon's sayings, which he had often wanted to quote while never dreaming that so perfect an opportunity would be afforded him. He remembered it. "You remind me," he said, "of a saying by Bacon, the great Bacon, that 'a much-talking judge is like an ill-tuned cymbal.'" "You are offensive, sir!" cried the judge. "We both are," Smith replied; "the difference is that I'm trying to be, and you can't help it. I who have been listened to with respect by the highest tribunal in the land am not going to be browbeaten by a garrulous old county court judge."[14]

One must learn not to be impatient and also to laugh when the tables are turned against him. This is well illustrated in an incident which the late Emory R. Buckner, a great trial lawyer, told at his own expense:

I remember when offering a bill of lading in a prosecution . . . it was objected to because I described the paper as a bill of lading, whereas the paper spoke for itself; I, impatient and not waiting as I should have for a ruling, promptly broke in with "Why, your Honor, I have a perfect right to describe generally the paper I am introducing, otherwise the jury might think it is a barn door." My opponent immediately replied, "I beg to disagree with the learned District Attorney, as I am sure the jury will consider the paper a darn bore." This caused a laugh at my expense and diverted the mind of the jury from the main facts which was altogether a mistake. The objection was overruled.[15]

One more example must suffice. Mr. A and Mr. B, whom I mentioned earlier, were arguing a case in which Mr. B appeared for Mr. C. At the end of Mr. B's summation one of Mr. C's partners arose and made the extraordinary statement that when the case came into their office he and his young associates had studied it and had become convinced of its merits. Then they referred it to Mr. C himself, who likewise reached the same conclusion, and Mr. C would be trying it himself were he not engaged elsewhere. Mr. A arose and then instead of objecting, as he well might have to this extraordinary statement on the ground that it violated the Canons of Professional Ethics, contented himself by repeating in mock seriousness the offensive remarks, adding that when he heard them he thought he had better retire from the case, but suddenly he recalled that he had learned in his college days that sometimes even Homer nods. These few words, uttered with impish gravity, made Mr. C and all the members of his law firm seem quite ridiculous, as indeed they deserved to.

It is these unexpected encounters that give zest to a trial. Men of great wit like Joseph H. Choate have a great advantage. I have often wondered if anyone today could have matched him when there were women on the jury. He was once asked if he had another life to lead what he would like to be and he instantly replied, "Mrs. Choate's second husband." His wit was always effortless, an outpouring of a lively mind. There can be no doubt but that a large part of the success of the masters of the forensic arena is due to the fact, not that they have keen minds, but that they know the rules of the game so thoroughly that they never have to worry about what is to be done next. All they have to do is to keep their minds on the play and remember the power of brevity and clarity, of wit and humor, of tenacity and courage.

TRAINING FOR ADVOCACY

In analyzing the component parts of the several types of forensic persuasion, I have had to do what the botanist does when he pulls apart a beautiful flower in order to describe it scientifically. No analysis or description of forensic address or of a flower can catch the full spirit of the living thing. A knowledge of its component parts, however, is an indispensable preliminary to knowing the living whole. We progress best, moreover, if we know the science before we attempt to learn the art. How does one go about being an advocate? I have already indicated the six factors in every lawyer's life, all of which need to be cultivated in high degree by the advocate. I have dwelt on the fact that every art requires practice, and I have mentioned regretfully the relative lack of good examples and the extreme abundance of bad examples in our courts today, due to our lack of training in the arts of advocacy and our preoccupation with office practice.

Though styles may change, the prerequisites for advocacy do not—high ideals of personal conduct, the development of all of one's faculties to a state of coordinated perfection, an abiding interest in one's fellow man and in the solution of the great problems of the day, a willingness to accept the call to public

service and to go through the arduous work of preparation
therefor for years before the call comes, an appreciation of the
great thoughts and aspirations of the past and the present,
and of course practice, practice, and then more practice.

NOTES

INTRODUCTION

1. *Time* 56 (April 10, 1978).
2. Quoted in *The Reporter* 17 (February 1978).
3. "When he was ninety Wendell Holmes would quote that phrase, adding that his father had kicked him upstairs into the law and he supposed he should be grateful." C. Bowen, *Yankee from Olympus* 201 (1944).
4. *Op. cit. supra* note 1.
5. D. Malone, *Jefferson the Virginian* 69 (1948).
6. R. Haskett, "Village Clerk and Country Lawyer: William Paterson's Legal Experience, 1763–1772," 66 *Proceedings of the New Jersey Historical Society* 155, 160 (1948).
7. G. Dunne, *Justice Joseph Story and the Rise of the Supreme Court* 34 (1970).
8. C. Bowen, *The Lawyer and the King's English* 11 (Brandeis Lawyers' Society, 1951).
9. *Op. cit. supra* note 3, at 207.
10. *Ibid.*, 204.
11. J. Lash, *From the Diaries of Felix Frankfurter* 4 (1975).
12. F.L. Bailey, *For the Defense* 11 (1975).
13 F. Maitland, *English Law and the Renaissance* 18, 25 (Rede Lecture, 1901).

14. See A. Vanderbilt II, *Changing Law: A Biography of Arthur T. Vanderbilt* (1976); F. Klein and J. Lee, *Selected Writings of Arthur T. Vanderbilt* (1965); E. Gerhart, *Arthur T. Vanderbilt: The Compleat Counsellor* (1980).

PRELEGAL EDUCATION

This chapter is part of a "Report on Prelegal Education" written by Arthur T. Vanderbilt for the Section of Legal Education and Admissions to the Bar of the American Bar Association. It was approved by the American Bar Association and Association of American Colleges as "a masterful statement of the basic issues that concern the development of an adequate prelegal course in college. It will long be accepted as an authoritative presentation of . . . the essentials of prelegal education." Quoted in "A Report on Prelegal Education," 25 *N.Y.U. Law Review* 200, 202 (1950).

1. S. Neumann, *Permanent Revolution* (1942).
2. Holmes, *The Path of the Law (Collected Legal Papers)* 173 (1920).
3. W. Keener, 1 *Yale L.J.* 146.
4. Holmes, *The Common Law* 1 (1881).
5. Stone, Clark, and Llewellyn quotations from *A.A.L.S. Handbook* 134 (1932).
6. *Op. cit. supra* note 6, at 133.
7. I *Select Essays in Anglo-American Legal History* 839–840.
8. V. P. Ford, *The Writings of Thomas Jefferson* 298–301 (1904).
9. *Ibid.*, VI at 71.
10. *Ibid.*, at 72–73.
11. X *Works of John Adams* 104–105 (1856).
12. *Miscellaneous Writings of Joseph Story* 527–528 (1852).
13. *Ibid.*, at 528–529.
14. I.W. Story, *Life and Letters of Joseph Story* 74 (1851).
15. A *Treatise on the Study of Law* 67–68 (1797).
16. *Ibid.*, at 55, 57.

STUDYING LAW

1. J. Osborn, Jr., *The Paper Chase* 6–9 (1971).
2. 372 *U.S.* 391 (1963).
3. W. Douglas, *Go East, Young Man* 146 (1974).
4. *Ibid.*, 164.

5. As author and first-year Harvard Law School student Scott Turow prepared his schedule of courses for the second semester, he made his selection with one principle in mind: " . . . that I would not submit myself again to a teacher who ran his classroom like the Star Chamber. I did not care if a professor was known as the greatest formulator of the law since Hammurabi—if he was said to treat his students harshly, I passed him by." S. Turow, *One L* 275 (1977).

6. 84 *N.H.* 114, 146 A. 641 (1929).

7. *Op. cit. supra* note 5, at 294.

8. I. F. Lee, *New Jersey as a Colony and as a State* 308 (1903).

9. J. Nortrup, "The Education of a Western Lawyer," 12 *Am J. Leg. His.* 294 (1968).

10. C. Langdell, *A Selection of Cases on the Law of Contracts* vii (1871).

11. Quoted in L. Friedman, *A History of American Law* 532 (1973).

12. *Centennial History of the Harvard Law School 1817–1917* 35 (1918).

13. *Op. cit. supra* note 11, at 533.

14. For a detailed history of the development of legal education in the United States, see R. Stevens, "Two Cheers for 1870: The American Law School," reprinted in D. Fleming and B. Bailyn, *Law in American History* (1971).

15. A. Reed, *Training for the Public Profession of the Law* 371 (1921).

16. J. Redlich, *The Common Law and the Case Method* 40 (1920).

17. J. Goebel, *A History of the School of Law, Columbia University* 144 (1955).

18. J. Lash, *Fron the Diaries of Felix Frankfurter* 4 (1975).

19. *Op cit. supra* note 3, at 174.

20. R. Haskett, "Village Clerk and Country Lawyer: William Paterson's Legal Experience, 1763–1772," 66 *Proceedings of the New Jersey Historical Society* 155, 160 (1948).

21. I. A. Beveridge, *The Life of John Marshall* 159–160 (1916).

22. L. Baker, *John Marshall: A Life in Law* 66 (1974).

23. M. Belli, *My Life on Trial* 60 (1976).

24. J. Story, *The Value and Importance of Legal Studies* (1829).

25. *Op. cit. supra* note 23, at 46.

26. G. Sharswood, *Memoir of William Blackstone* (1860).

27 F. Rodell, *Woe Unto You, Lawyers!* 22 (1957).

28. *Time* 58 (April 10; 1978).

29. *Op. cit. supra* note 5, at 57–58.

30. H. Black, Jr., *My Father: A Remembrance* 117 (1975).

31 Quoted in R. Speidel, R. Summers, J. White, *Commercial and Consumer Law* xviii (1974).

32. W. B. Raushenbush, "Two Tips on Writing Law School Examinations," 4 (American Bar Association, 1962).

33. *Op. cit. supra* note 23, at 59.

34. *Ibid.*

35. Kaufman, "Does the Judge Have a Right to Qualified Counsel?" 61 *A.B.A.J.* 570 (1975).

36. H. Cecil, *Brief to Counsel* 66 (1958).

37. J. Goulden, *The Super-Lawyers* 74–75 (1972).

38. Burger, "The State of the Judiciary—1975," 61 *A.B.A.J.* 439 (1975).

39. *Op. cit. supra* note 28, at 56.

40. M. Cohen, *Legal Research in a Nutshell* 1 (1971).

41. D. Danelski and J. Tulchin (eds.), *The Autobiographical Notes of Charles Evans Hughes* 59 (1973).

42. W. Story, *Life and Letters of Joseph Story* 74 (1851).

43. B. Schwartz, *The Law in America* 305–306 (1974).

THE ART OF ADVOCACY

This chapter is reprinted from "Forensic Persuasion," the 1950 John Randolph Tucker Lecture delivered at Washington and Lee University by Arthur T. Vanderbilt.

1. *Law and Public Opinion in England During the Nineteenth Century* 19–20 (1905).

2. Address in *Report, Fiftieth Annual Meeting of the Maryland State Bar Association* 190, at 201, 203 (1949).

3. Address at the Sixth Conference of the Inter-American Bar Association, Edison Institute, Dearborn, Michigan, May 24, 1949.

4. Frankfurter and Hart, "Business of the Supreme Court at the October Term, 1934" 49 *Harv. L. Rev.* 68, 107 (1935).

5. Parry, *The Seven Lamps of Advocacy* 78 (1924).

6. "Some Observations on the Art of Advocacy," in *Law and Other Things* 200, at 203–204 (1937). Cf. as to duty of lawyers to disclose to courts any adverse decisions, 35 *A.B.A.J.* 876 (1949).

7. S. Bartlett in *Speeches* 41, at 43 (1913).
8. *Op. cit. supra* note 5, at 65–66.
9. *Self-Cultivation in English* 15 (1897).
10. *Modern Homes Inc.* v. *Atlas Assurance Co.*, 108 Atl. 869, 870 (N.J. Sup. Ct. 1919).
11. Hoar, "Some Historical Reminiscences," 25 *Scrib. Mag.* 285, 290 (1899).
12. G. Shattuck in *Speeches* 70, at 72 (1913).
13. Majoribanks, *For the Defence* 235 (1929).
14. Roberts (Ephesian), *Lord Birkenhead* 101–102, 103–104, 104–105 (1927).
15. "The Lawyer in Court," 27 *A.B.A.J.* 5, 7 (1941).

INDEX

For a complete list of books available from Penguin in the United States, write to Dept. DG, Penguin Books, 299 Murray Hill Parkway, East Rutherford, New Jersey 07073.

For a complete list of books available from Penguin in Canada, write to Penguin Books Canada Limited, 2801 John Street, Markham, Ontario L3R 1B4.